The Dragon, The Witch and The Thirteen

The Dragon, The Witch
and
The Thirteen

Book 2 of The Fae Sagas

by
Flora-Beth Edwards

The Dragon, The Witch and The Thirteen

Text copyright©2021 Flora-Beth Edwards
Cover images courtesy of GoGraph.com
Design©2021 Ribeiro

ISBN 978-1-8380247-5-8
ISSN 2752-5694

The Author has asserted her rights under the Copyright, Designs and Patents Act 1988 to be identified as the author of this work.

This book is a work of fiction and any resemblance of characters therein to persons living or dead is purely coincidental.

Neither fairies nor other magical creatures have been discombobulated during the writing and production of this book.

Conditions of Sale

No part of this book may be reproduced or transmitted by any means without the permission of the publisher.

British Library Cataloguing in Publication Data.

A catalogue record for this book is available from the British Library.

1 3 5 4 2

Printed and bound in Great Britain by CPI Group (UK) Ltd.

Hawkwood Books 2021

Dedicated to all those who still believe

in the magic of this world.

CONTENTS

1. The Tide Turns 1
2. The Buttercup Ring 12
3. Elemental Orbs 18
4. The Wych Elms 26
5. The White Crane 32
6. The Lady Aethelflaed 37
7. The Dark Fae and The Wolf 43
8. The Path 53
9. The Forest 60
10. Out of the Dark and Into the Light 64
11. The Bridge 72
12. The Quadruple Crossroads 79
13. Dragon Fire 90
14. The Immortals 99
15. The Castle and The Mermaid 104
16. The Castle Secrets 109
17. Dragon Ride 115
18. The High Priestess 120
19. Sailing 125
20. Loch Leven 132
21. The Lady Rises 138
22. Lammas Fair 145
23. Appendix 151/i
24. Illustrations xix

1. The Tide Turns

Professor Riley held out his hand to Ava who stood before him. She shone as bright as the sun for she was bathed in a shimmering shower of gold and illuminated the vast empty space around her father. The darkness turned upon itself as shadows ran from the light.

Her warmth and her love gave grace in the power she came from. Fire and spirit merged into human form as passion and water made whole within magic.

A hideous screech echoed out of the depths as evil had awoken once more. Professor Riley turned from searching the black emptiness and desperately reached out to Ava. He shuddered as tiny sparks of electricity tingled through him as their fingers finally met but no sooner had they touched than Ava faded away into dancing sparks of light.

The hideous screech turned into a mocking, cackling laugh with clicks and deep grunts which bellowed from the belly of the earth.

Professor Riley shut his eyes tight at the horrific sound. His hands clenched into fists as strength and defiance welled up inside him.

"You won't win this battle for we will never surrender this earth to you," he shouted into the darkness.

The cackling formed non-human sounds, vicious in their anger, spitting words like venom.

"What battle? This earth is already mine," echoed the voice as it resonated around the Professor with hideous bouts of laughter. Horrible images formed as the voice disappeared into the darkness, of earthquakes shattering buildings, cities on fire, floods devasting coastlines and icebergs crumbling into the oceans.

Professor Riley closed his eyes once more and covered his ears with his hands as he dropped to his knees before shouting, "NEVER!"

Ava awoke with a jolt. She sprang upright in bed immediately as her eyes opened waking Jennifer who stretched out her paws and yawned. Her paws almost touched Ava's pillow.

Ava gently ruffled her fur.

"Oh, I know Jen, I dreamt of dad again."

Jennifer raised her head attentively to look at Ava before collapsing on her side and returned to sleep. Tutting, Ava scrambled out of bed pulling the covers on top of Jennifer.

"Oh, you're no help."

Jennifer leapt off the bed before Ava had slipped her feet into flip flops as she knew what that meant… breakfast. Her paws padded the oak floorboards of Candlesby Manor and she was at the door before Ava had finished putting her feet into her flip flops. As she passed the mirror she gasped, her hair was a tangled mass, elflocks galore! She shrugged her shoulders and continued walking.

As Ava opened the door, the smell of bacon, sausages, eggs, toast and coffee wafted through the levels of the house to her room.

"Tarran!" Ava exclaimed as she raced Jennifer down the stairs to the kitchen, but by the third level Jennifer was winning. Ava had an idea. Gripping the bannister, she popped her leg over the rail and promptly slid down. She waved as she passed Jennifer.

Since the events of Midsummer, Ava had changed a lot and no longer feared such small things as sliding down bannisters. After all, she could manipulate time and could have won the race by doing so now. Maybe that would have been wiser, for she had no idea how to stop. She had picked up pace, speeding down at an alarming rate. The large wooden newel post was looming mencingly closer.

She closed her eyes and braced herself for impact, but her body zipped off the end of the bannister, catapulting her through the air. She was ready to crash land when she bounced on something soft and delicate, moist to the touch like sparkling drops of mist.

Below her were delicate folds of what looked like a giant white marshmallow.

"The Cloud of Believing!" she exclaimed.

"Yes, Ava, just as I am ordered to keep you safe, so too is every being in Fae, commanded by their majesties – remember his majesty the King's decree in the throne room on your first trip to Avalonia?"

Commander George of the faery realm was walking past, his head in a book, at just the right moment. He was wearing small round spectacles that sat on the end of his nose and a teaching gown from the university of Fae. He almost looked human, were it not for his peculiar dapper attire and his sparkling complexion.

"Oh yes, how could I possibly forget?" replied Ava, clambering off the cloud.

Jennifer reached the bottom of the stairs and Ava bent down, ruffling the clouds wisps that gave a pleasing shake like a wagging tail before speeding up again, out of site. Jennifer held her nose high in the air and sniffed indignantly as she gracefully bounced towards the kitchen like a show dog at Crufts.

"Well George," said Ava, "what have we got planned for today?"

"More study and research, my lady."

Ava gave out a groan as she turned towards the breakfast room, but her eyes lit up as she entered. The table was full of delicious dishes each with an intoxicating aroma. Amongst the bacon and sausages were plates of pancakes, syrup, bowls of blueberries, strawberries, bananas, croissants, brioches, jams, marmalades, fresh orange juice, not to mention coffee and teas and the obligatory basket of chocolate which held pride of place on the table - a centre piece piled high into a mouth watering mountain.

Several aunts sat round the table, already tucking into the fabulous fare, but the biggest plate was Morgan's. On seeing Ava, his eyes widened and he muttered with his mouth full,

"Here Ava," and he patted the next chair..

Pulling up the chair alongside him she asked,

"Hello Morgan. What's good? I'm sure you've tried most of it already."

"Everything," Morgan replied as he tucked into the sausage bun he had made himself.

Tarran came in with another plate of toast.

"Good morning princess, what will you have?"

Although everything looked delicious, something was missing. The dream of her father had unsettled Ava terribly. Scratching her elflocks, she replied,

"What I really fancy, you don't seem to have made."

The room fell silent and Morgan stopped eating.

"Oh!"

Tarran, disappointed, did not know what to say.

Anxious not to upset him, Ava added,

"Let me see… It does look lovely, I must say. I'm sorry, Tarran, bad dreams. I'venot quite woken up yet. This is a wonderful spread."

"That's his third plate," Aunt Fawn chipped in. "You should have seen what he ate first."

They all laughed, knowing that Tarran was famous for his appetite. Yet he was an active boy so he could eat till the cows came home and never put on weight, so quite often, he did.

Aunt Winifred came in. Like all Ava's aunts, she had a presence and a mystery about her. You would not want to cross her.

"Good morning niece," she said tenderly as she bent down and kissed Ava on the forehead. Holding up a piece of Ava's hair complete with elflocks, she simply uttered, "My goodness!"

"Good morning, auntie."

Aunt Winifred stared knowingly at her niece. Winifred had a way of seeing into her niece, and into others, a kind of mind reading. She was wise and perceptive and there was very little chance of keeping secrets from her.

"Still dreaming about him?" she asked, sitting down beisde Ava. "It would be a pity if you didn't," she added. "He is your father and means everything to you. What kind of daughter would you be if you did not miss him and want him back? So many of the things we worry about come to us in dreams. Keep dreaming, Ava, all will be well and he will return."

Other aunts appeared. Lexi and Ellie came in with a huge plate of eggs, scrambled, boiled and poached, and a bowl full of freshly picked summer flowers for George who, upon seeing the delicious array, dropped the books, gown and spectacles and transformed into the magical being he truly was before diving in to gorge himself on the flowers, throwing nasturtiums and poppies into the air.

Aunt Ellie ignored him and said, "You know Ava, it would be nice to have some fish on the menu. I could do my speciality gumbo. Everyone likes that."

The aunts agreed.

"Winnie," said Lexi, "why don't we go down to the seaside for the day and get some?"

"Oh yes please Winnie! Perhaps we could gather some samphire while we're there, or is it too early?"

"Too early Ellie," replied Winifred. "It's an August speciality, but a day out at the seaside would be a welcome break. What do you think Professor Wrenn, do you think we could play hooky for the day?"

George popped his fairy head up from the flower bowl and tried to be serious, but with flowers falling from his head it didn't quite have the desired impact.

"Well, the children do need their education and school must carry on," he replied in all seriousness.

Morgan, Ava and Tarran were in glorious sync as they groaned, "Nooo!"

"Oh, George," said Lexi, "we know that education is important. However, Ava will learn far more by practising her skills than sitting behind a desk. Magic is to be experienced, not learned from a book. And we need time to think about the next treasure."

"True, true," mused George. "Perhaps we could all do with a bit of a break. After all, we have been hitting the books quite hard," he laughed, flying back to his seat at the table, transforming into human form once again, wearing a striped boating blazer of cream and pink with matching cotton trousers and tan Oxfords, all topped off with a walking cane and panama hat.

"I'll have a ninety-nine with a flake please," said Morgan, staring at George.

Ava put her hand to her mouth to cover her sniggers. Tarran chipped in, "I'll have sprinkles on mine," before falling into fits of giggles.

On hearing the mockery, George straightened his jacket indignantly.

"I have it on good authority, you know, that I am one of the best dressers in Avalonia. Indeed, I am regarded as a key figure in the Avalonia New Wave movement."

With that, George clicked his fingers and muttered a simple garment transformation spell.

Ava, Tarran and Morgan all found themselves wearing beautiful, quirky clothes inspired with a seaside style from the 1920s.

Morgan raised his hand to his head and found he was wearing a straw boating hat whilst Tarran looked smart in his white Daks slack trousers and yellow striped short sleeved polo shirt and tan Oxfords.

Morgan and Tarran surveyed each other with a mixture of astonishment and admiration.

Ava was twirling round, trying to get to grips with her navy and cream-flowered wide-legged beach pyjama trousers. Her hair had miraculously turned from an elf locked manifestation to a braided updo entwined with forget-me-nots.

The three of them looked like a picture postcard from a long forgotten past but with something extra special added. The clothes were of course magical, made of a cloth Ava did not recognise.

"What material is this?" she asked.

"All natural, Ava. Yours is a collection of white lily petals and navy morning glory whilst master Morgan's trousers are a mixture of wide-wale rhubarb leaves topped with an oak leaf belt and a pheasant feather sport shirt with desert boots of birch bark. Finally, master Tarran's Daks slacks are made of shed snakeskin and his polo shirt of beech leaves with a sycamore stand-up collar. Oh, and his Oxfords are woven from the purest pigeon and pheasant feathers. It is, my dear girl, the Avalonian New Wave – and you're welcome."

Ellie clapped her hands.

"Oh my, you all look totally scrumptious. Well done, Commander George, you've outdone yourself this time."

"Indeed, well said, Ellie. Come on then my little fairy seaside bunch, let's go," Aunt Winifred instructed.

"Where are we off too, Winnie?" asked Lexi.

"We need to commune with the Seven Sisters... that's you, me, Ellie..." Aunt Winifred turned to the other aunts and continued, "Fawn, Brenna are you up for a trip to the beach?"

"Yes, of course," replied Aunt Fawn, gracefully rising from her chair with Aunt Brenna following.

"Excellent. That leaves two more. Tarran dear boy, what's your mother up to?"

"Working the night shift, so not available," Tarran replied, looking to the floor while mumbling, "She sends her apologies in advance though. She had a feeling something special was going to happen."

"Well, of course she would, Tarran," said Winifred. "She is a Thirteen after all. Now, who's up for a lovely trip to the seaside, my style?"

All hands went up in the air.

"Briar and Holly, you are requested on our trip. April, Guinevere and Eowyn, you're on guard duty. Watch the house and book. When Meadow finishes her shift at the hospital, she can keep watch too. Make no mistake ladies, the war has begun. Keep your wits about you."

April, Guinevere and Eowyn bowed respectively to Winifred.

"The rest of us - let's saddle up!"

"Saddle up? Are we riding a horse?" Morgan asked in between mouthfuls of yet more sausage.

"Don't you ever stop eating?" Tarran asked him, shaking his head.

"No, he doesn't. He's a bottomless pit. Get up boy," Aunt Ellie told him.

"No Morgan," said Winifred, "not horses, but the next best thing, our motorbikes."

"Oh wow, can I have my own? I…"

"No, you may not!" came a sharp reply from his mother who didn't even let him finish the sentence.

"Ellie you ride with me in the side car. Brenna, you have Tarran, Holly you have Morgan. Ride front and centre ladies. Briar lead and Fawn take up the rear, Lexi centre. Commander Wrenn you have Ava."

"You don't ride a motorbike, you're a fairy!" exclaimed Ava, flabbergasted.

"Oh Ava, haven't you learned anything yet?" George replied, snapping his fingers and turning into a motorbike rider from the 1920s, complete with goggles.

"Perfect George," Brenna commented while giggling with Fawn before giving her a kiss.

Holly took Ava's arm.

"How exciting, Ava! I get to go on an adventure with you at last."

"I don't think so Aunt Holly, it's just a trip to the seaside."

"Ava, dear Ava! George is right. When are you ever

went round it three times, then continued down the path. As they turned onto the main road, the bikes morphed into bright beams of light. Ava could see the world around her and her aunts including Tarran and Morgan riding on the back of the bikes, but they were encased within a large translucent bubble.

She could see the world passing by with people in cars, but the people apparently didn't see them. All that could be seen were a bunch of little elemental orbs floating down the motorway.

In fact, most people would either never have seen them or not realised what they were seeing. They would have appeared as flashes of light in the rear-view mirror, a trick of reflected sunlight.

It is not uncommon. People as a rule do not see magic around them, being too busy with their daily lives, but the fae world is flashing and orbing here, there and everywhere.

In no time at all, Ava found herself riding up to the seaside. The motorbikes slowed down and the world around her took shape.

The Flying Squirrel came to a stop and George took his goggles off.

"Wow, wasn't that fun?"

"How did we get here so fast George?"

"Have you forgotten fairy speed? I think you need another trip to Avalonia," George suggested while raising one eyebrow.

Tarran and Morgan clambered off their bikes and Aunt

Winifred helped Ellie out the side car. As she brushed herself down, she said to Ava,

"Right then, would you like to meet my great grandmother?"

Ava wrinkled her forehead.

"She's still alive?"

Tarran looked to the heavens.

"You really don't know much, do you," he said, "for a summer spent in books."

Ellie wrapped her arm round Ava.

"Come along Ava, let's go to the museum. Tarran, you too. Morgan come and meet your great, great grandmother."

The boys glanced at one another, raising eyebrows. The thought of spending a day in a museum filled them with dread, even Tarran who would have normally loved the idea but not when the aunts were going to perform magic.

"We'll meet you at the Seven Sisters, Ellie, at noon," said Holly.

Tarran was curious.

"What are they up to?"

Ellie whispered, "You'll see."

Ava wrinkled her forehead; she had that diamond shape again between her eyebrows.

"They're up to something Ava," Morgan whispered as the quartet walked on to the museum.

George had transformed himself into a seagull, flying alongside. He soared high to get a better look at the area.

The museum was the standard run-of-the-mill type

which housed antique postcards and Victorian seaside memorabilia. A nostalgic trip through life before, during and after the war.

Ellie led the way to a room which was empty except for one plinth. Placed in a glass cabinet was a replica of a skull and the face of reconstructed woman.

"Ava, allow me to introduce my great grandmother. You all know her as the Beachy Head Woman, but her name is Amara, which means grace. She is from West Africa and we call her Mama."

Ava leaned in closer to the inscription and read aloud:

Beachy Head Woman
First discovered in 1956-1959. The Beachy Head Woman lived during the Roman period around 200 – 250 AD. She is thought to have originated from Sub-Saharan Africa.

During forensic facial reconstruction, several tests, including isotope analysis, revealed the Beachy Head Woman grew up in Southeast England.

Ava stood silently until Tarran said, "Wow Ellie, I always thought you were from Jamaica. Your name, I mean, being…"

"Windrush?" Aunt Ellie finished the sentence, shaking her head. "That is part of the myth of the Windrush population. Yes, the majority came from the Caribbean on the ex-troopship Empire Windrush, but others were from England and even Mexico."

"So, did your family leave England then, Ellie?" Tarran inquired.

Ellie grew silent then answered quietly.

"The war changed everything, children. It destroyed so much."

"The war, do you mean World War II?" Ava asked.

"Yes, so much evil, so many battles. I fled to Trinidad after it."

Tarran had started to do some maths in his head.

"The war was over 80 years ago. Ellie, how old are you?"

"Witches, dear Tarran, and especially members of The Thirteen, can live for nearly 500 years."

"Did you know all of this?" Ava asked Morgan who looked like he knew everything.

"Aye, of course. My mother is a member of The Thirteen and a powerful witch in her own right. This is my family Ava, just as you are."

Ava's wrinkled forehead formed into the diamond again. Tarran's eyes squinted as if he had been pierced by something. He knew what that diamond meant.

"So, Ellie, when did you leave for Trinidad?"

"Just after the war - and that night."

"That night?"

"The night of the great battle when your great grandmother Evelyn closed the clocktower forever."

"Was it an air raid?"

Ellie pressed her lips together and widened her eyes, "Mmm, you might call it that."

Tarran, Ava, and Morgan stared at each other before Ava replied.

"What else would you call it? I thought it had been a big storm."

"Yes, indeed it was Ava," answered George who had bounded in wearing his human form before Ellie could reply. He was wearing his turquoise striped blazer with white slacks and tan Oxfords. His fairy features stood out with his sharp pixie-ish lines and edges. His bright blue eyes shone as clearly as his skin which had an air of starlight about it, whilst his blonde short hair was gelled, giving the appearance of it being even sleeker.

At times, George did not blend well into the human world despite his best efforts. There was no mistaking him, he was truly a magical being on loan from Fae.

"It was a storm like no other, and one which set events in motion which we are dealing with today. Evil emerged that night with the arrival of the enemy into this world, not to mention," George turned his head in disgust and sniffed, "that ghastly Robin Goodfellow, beginning his campaign of hate. Now ladies and gents, enough history, we really must be going. My lady Elizabeth Windrush, the sisters are beginning. We need to return to the others."

"Come along children," ordered Ellie, "we need to go," and she ushered out the now surprisingly intrigued Ava, Tarran and Morgan.

3. Elemental Orbs

Although they were some distance away from the cliffs, they could hear a chanting sound carried on the breeze. The five stood to listen as the world went on around them. Nobody seemed to hear it. Morgan spoke softly.

"It's magic Ava, feel it, see it, believe it."

"Commander George, you take Ava please. Boys you come with me," instructed Ellie.

The party of five splintered off and went their separate ways. Tarran turned back round to Ava, shrugged his shoulders and carried on walking behind Ellie and Morgan.

Ava watched them until they were out of sight. She raised one eyebrow.

"George, what's going on?"

"They have to awaken the Seven Sisters. The world needs our help more than anything now and we need to find that next treasure before Lammas. Come along, the beach is this way."

Ava's diamond formed again. She had learned to go along with it but she was also learning to trust her instincts and something that July day did not feel right.

George walked soldierly beside her as they ventured towards the beach. The haze on the horizon flickered in the distance. The world appeared milky and stretched. Ava glanced at the passing people but no one seemed to see her.

At the beach, she kicked her shoes off as did George. They walked towards the water's edge and paddled their feet as they continued along towards the cliffs. The mysterious chanting grew louder and little glowing orbs darted here and there. Ava followed them as they seemed to dance through the air.

She glanced up to the sky and watched the clouds, the wisps of cumulus fractus morphed into shapes that resembled letters like an elongated 'V'. She tried to remember her faeroglyphs. The 'V' preceded a long wispy cloud that looked like a sword, a flaming sword in a seamless cloudless sky. These two shapes appeared in the instant swallows darted in front of her and the breeze swirled around.

George grabbed her arm as the world fell silent. Even the sound of the sea disappeared - waves broke along the shore in appalling silence. She felt the breeze but could no longer hear the rustling of wind.

The two of them glanced round the beach. It was the height of summer, schools had finished and people should have been revelling at the water's edge. But no sound.

But there were no heaving masses, hardly anyone, only a handful of people had ventured out to enjoy a day at the beach. The ice-cream van that sat near the beach had no endless queue. And all was quiet.

The children who played at the water's edge wore face masks. The Fairground on the pier was empty except for one or two girls who flirted with the attendants behind the big wheel, their smiles hid from view by masks of many colours. Silently.

The world seemed tired and old. What little fun the people had seemed forced, and tinged with fear. A fear they could not explain. How could they? They did not know the face of the enemy. The unseen force that had invaded their world, wrecking their future. Still and silent.

The wind changed and a cold breeze seemed to whip around from nowhere. People ran from the sea to the cover of their beach towels. Few had ventured out on this July day but they all ran for shelter.

Since Ava had found the first treasure, the enemy had increased its waves of attack on humanity. Was this yet another battle about to erupt? Ava listened intently. She heard the soft sound of dried seaweed drifting along the sand, like tiny hooves galloping across the beach. It rolled along the dunes, up and down, bouncing and skipping. Ava's eyes followed it.

All around, there was an imprisoning order. The pier rides had a booking time to limit the number of people at any one time. The world was in lockdown and life might never be the same again. Control and responsibility had become peoples' constant companion.

"George... is this real?"

"We are being shown one possible future Ava, what might happen if the enemy wins."

"Where is everyone?"

"There aren't many humans left after the final battle and the enemy is showing us what it has in store for those that remain."

The tiny, tinny sound of hooves grew louder but this this time there was no dried seaweed making it.

Ava heard the chanting on the breeze again as she

followed the sound towards the cliffs.

On top of each of the Seven Sisters stood an aunt, chanting with her arms raised in a 'V' shape like that she had seen in the sky.

A loud cracking sound shattered the silence. Ava held on to George tightly.

The earth felt as if it was moving and the sea swelled alarmingly. The cliffs split open like a giant mouth growing wider and wider. Ava could see a huge wave rolling towards them.

"We should run George," she yelled, but George remained rooted and still.

"No Ava, we are right where we need to be. No harm will come to a child of Fae."

"But..."

"Look."

George calmly pointed to the wave. Ava could see inside it. All manner of life was inside. Every fish, dolphin, even whale - every species could be seen riding inside the wave which had changed shape into an arrow. The cliffs grew wider like a monster yawning as the arrow wave now aimed for the mouth, crashing into it with a massive explosion. The cliffs closed round the wave, encasing every living species of the sea within the safety of the earth.

Except one.

The tiny hoof-tappings started again, but with each step they grew heavier and louder until at last they had grown into a pounding beat, no longer sprightly nor light.

These steps belonged to a beast.

Ava looked towards the aunts, still chanting with their hands reaching towards the universe. Morgan stood behind his mother and Tarran was standing with Aunt Winifred.

The heavy steps stopped pounding across the sand and Ava felt something breathing down her neck - a warm breath that was strong and moved her hair across her face. She closed her eyes, turned, and swallowed as she opened them again.

Towering in front of her was a dragon, its scales a dazzlingly green, its eyes ablaze. The most wonderful, awful, overwhelmingly terrifying sight.

"Ah," said George, "there you are! My lady Ava, may I introduce the greatest of all sea dragons, Protector of the House Seton, King Samphire," and, unbelievably, he reached out to stroke the huge animal who nudged closer to him, blinking several times.

"Ss... Samphire?" stuttered Ava. "Seton... isn't Morgan a Seton from his father?"

"Yes, he is, and my old friend King Samphire must have felt his presence, especially with the Protection Ark Ceremony?"

"Protection Ark Ceremony?" asked Ava as she took courage to stroke Samphire. The dragon raised his head slightly to one side so she could scratch under his chin.

"Yes, the Protection Ark Ceremony - when the world opens up to protect its own. All those animals you saw are envoys of their species, representatives of the sea."

The others came down from the cliffs. Tarran had his mouth wide open and Morgan had a huge smile running across his face.

King Samphire turned round and, on seeing Morgan, bowed his head. Morgan, in turn, bowed his head to his family's dragon.

"Samphire, my old friend. How are you mon petite douce?" Ellie exclaimed patting his scales. "You still like chasing the seaweed I see?"

Samphire wrinkled his nose as if he were smiling. Tarran in the meantime was still gobsmacked.

"It's a dragon… a real dragon… I mean!"

"Aye, Tarran, we heard you the first time. He is a protector of my family."

"Oh," said Tarran, "so that's why you have a green dragon on your crest?"

"Aye! And the pentagram for… well… you know," Morgan replied, feeling rather smug, telling Tarran something he did not know.

"Wow! This is… magnificent. I love it here!"

"Yes, Tarran," said Winifred, "that's why we are trying to save it. Ava, did you see any shapes in the clouds?" she asked, urgently.

"Yes auntie, I saw the… the… erm… tin," Ava replied, finally remembering her faeroglyphs.

"Tin, like a flying bird shape, similar to a long 'V'?"

"Yes, Auntie."

"Tin?"

"Your lessons are paying off," said George, congratulating Ava.

"That means…" said Aunt Lexi.

"The Sword…" Aunt Fawn replied.

"The Flaming Sword of Rhyddech, forged in the Age of Dragon," added George, and all eyes turned to Samphire as Morgan and Ellie stroked and gently patted his scales.

"Right then troops, saddle up. Methinks the library is calling."

"And the secret room," added Tarran, his eyes glinting at Winifred.

"King Samphire, we are returning to Candlesby. You are most welcome to join us, but I think you will probably want to stay by the sea."

Samphire nestled closer to Morgan.

"Goodbye, my dear Samphire! I will see you again soon," whispered Morgan.

"I think you're in love Morgan," Ava teased, whilst the others looked on at the doting boy and beast.

Samphire turned, raced away, fading as he ran. The tiny hoof sound beat across the sand again towards the sea before an almighty splash could be heard, crashing into the water.

Tarran, Ava and Morgan watched as every so often a huge wave and splash could be heard and seen exploding in the sea but what was making the wave was invisible to human eyes. All Tarran could say was, "Wow! Oh wow! I saw a dragon!"

Ava wanted to be happy, but she shuddered. All she could think about was her father and how he loved stories of dragons.

She grew quiet on the journey home as she remembered

her father. He was all she had ever known. Her mother was non-existent in her life and although Aunt Winifred had told her who she really was, she still felt an emptiness, having never really met her. She wondered if she ever would.

George felt her silence as the motorbikes roared into Candlesby. He gently inquired, "My Lady?"

"I'm alright George. I need to be on my own for a bit. I think I will visit Grandmother Apple."

"Very well, my Lady Ava. Stay within the Wych Elm borders, though."

She walked towards the trees. Tarran took off his helmet and was about to call to Ava but George waved his hand to stop him and whispered a firm 'No!'

Tarran and Morgan both watched on as Ava walked towards Grandmother Apple, alone and deep in thought.

4. The Wych Elms

Ava waved her hand at the darting dragonflies. 'There seems to be an awful lot of them this year,' she thought, stepping carefully as they had decided to sit in the evening sun on the warm grass. Their red and blue bodies darted here and there in between the sun's rays.

Grandmother Apple stood at the far end of the garden looking for all intents and purposes like a dead tree, but as Ava approached, the tree bloomed into life, branches stretched out with buds, leaves sprouted, then flowers formed until finally a full beautiful apple tree stood before Ava, laden with fruit.

"Welcome child," a voice said, as Grandmother Apple appeared in the knots and twists of the old bark.

"Good evening, Grandmother."

"What ails you, child? I can see your energy is sad."

"My energy?"

"The colours that surround you. You are a dark blue and red at the moment when normally you are yellow and green."

"I keep thinking about my father. I wish I could see if he is alright. It's been weeks since I last saw him by the spell you gave."

Grandmother Apple gently curved one of her branches round Ava in a loving embrace.

"There, there child. Your father is strong and wise. He has a warrior's spirit. Reach up, take a fruit. It will help."

There was a wonderful variety of colours - crimsons,

emeralds and golden. Ava picked a giant ruby red.

"Perfect," said Grandmother Apple. "That's just the one I would have picked. I always like that one, he's my favourite."

Her eyes closed as she felt the weight of fruit lighten ever so slightly.

"Thank you. Do I do the same as before, cutting it in half by candlelight?"

"No, no. You can bite this one now and eat it."

"Oh!" Ava looked down towards the ground. "So, it's just... ordinary?"

"No child, look at me. Do I look ordinary? You will see your father again - but do not try to free him, and tell him never to look behind. Now eat, and follow the dragonflies."

Ava took a bite out of the sweet fruit. Juicy drips fell on to her chin. As she wiped it away, she noticed the dragonflies coming closer. She had never seen one up close, but this one was hardly normal - it had what looked like a head and face with a little helmet on. It gave a salute to Grandmother Apple and started to march fly with its other dragonfly soldiers. He was leading the others, not forgetting to bow to Ava.

"I think you'd better follow him child. He wants to show you something."

"But Grandmother, I have to stay within the Wych Elms."

"Yes, the elms of Scotland. And so you shall Ava. Now follow him, dragonfly Generals are not known for their patience."

The dragonfly General and his army flew towards the wych elms.

Ava was apprehensive as she approached the elms, all standing in a row like guardians that had been purposely placed there.

A tiredness came over her as a an enchanted fog fell throughout the trees – a fog with the power to transform a human into the tiniest dragonfly. Unlike the General and his soldiers, though, who were blood red, Ava's body turned ink blue. She saluted the General who saluted back, then the dragonfly army started its journey through the fog and wych elms.

Ava could feel her tiny heart beating fast as she fluttered her wings, but she was no gentle fluttering butterfly. She was a quick firing dragonfly like darting and dancing spitfire.

The army fly-marched quickly towards a dark swirling mass. The Nothingness.

The General and his troops moved in bullet formation, and right in the middle flew Ava. Penetrating the darkness, the flying army took a sharp left then a sharp right in what felt like a complicated maze. Ava kept in sync with the army, feeling the air around her getting heavier and heavier.

The army carried on to a circular building within this swirling mass of negativity and oppression. In the darkness, the dragonfly army was guided by a tiny light. They flew faster and faster towards it, their beating wings making a deep, hypnotic humming sound until they were upon the light, illuminating a tiny room.

Ava watched the light grow as they approached it.

"Daddy!" she cried, in her tiny, enchanted voice.

Professor Riley was curled up on the floor. As he heard the buzzing of tiny wings, he questioned what he was seeing before him.

"Ava?"

Rising to his feet, he felt the breeze of hundreds of these wonderful little wings around him.

"General Ignatius?" he said to the General who saluted him.

"Daddy, follow me! Come on, there's no time to lose!"

"Ava is that you?"

"Me!" Ava replied, flying closer to him.

Staring at his daughter, Professor Riley simply said, "Grandmother Apple?"

"Yes! Now come on, Dad, let's get you out of here. Follow me and don't look behind. General, onward!"

General Ignatius signalled to the rest of the army which swiftly turned around. Ava followed, this time with her father clambering behind, his efforts met with huge resistance from the swirling black mass of Nothingness. Every step he took was painful for a weary heaviness pulled him down and back, back and down.

He carried on though, following Ava, following her light. Even in her bewitched form, he knew the power inside her. She was a true daughter of Fae.

A loud screech ripped the air as the Nothingness realised its captive was escaping. Once more, Ava found herself amongst the wych elms of Candlesby, transformed back to human form.

"Come on Dad, just a few more feet and we're home free."

Her father reached out his hand to hers as the dragonflies created a wall of protection around them.

The screeching increased, unbearably loud and piercing.

"No Dad, no! Don't look behind! Please, keep facing me. Come on."

"How far is it from me Ava?"

"Far enough, Dad. Come on. Please. Don't look back."

The screeching echoed terribly as the Nothingness approached. Darkness was spreading across the land, encroaching on anything it touched, leaving decay and desolation in its wake.

Ava reached out her hand to her father, but the wych elms had transformed into the witches of the past, their trunks and branches now the arms and legs of ancient witches, hidden in the trees centuries before to escape the witch hunters.

Another blood-curdling screech.

The enemy was close. Too close.

"I love you, Sparks," said Professor Riley, "always remember that. I can do nothing for you now. You need your mother. Seek her. Find her."

Professor Riley turned round to face his enemy.

For Ava it felt like an eternity. Unintentionally, she had slowed time. As soon as he turned, she knew that all was lost. In an instant, there was a bright flash and the sound of air being sucked from the world which grew dark and cold.

An explosion of darkness pulsated round the sky.

Ava was thrown to the ground as the wych elms let go of her. The blast hit them, sending them once more into the trees. Ava could no longer hide the pain inside. She felt it burning like a flame until it reached her throat.

She let out a shattering scream.

Birds flew from their nests and a host of wild creatures came scurrying from their night's rest, frightened for their lives.

5. The White Crane

Commander George dropped the books in the library and before they hit the floor was at her side. Ava cried uncontrollably as George held her tight and rocked her to and fro.

Aunts Winifred, Lexi, Fawn and Brenna were first on the scene with Tarran and Meadow following behind as Ellie ran as best she could with her hand on her heart.

"Oh, my sweet child," said Ellie breathlessly.

Morgan was already running through the wych elms trying to entice the Nothingness back for a good fight but was stopped by General Ignatius.

George swept Ava's hair away from her face. His magical touch soothed the pain.

"Why can't things be as they once were?"

"Because my dear child, life is forever moving, seasons come and go and that includes us. We are nothing more than leaves on the breeze, carried along on the winds of time. As we are tossed and turned through life, we see and feel many great things. Stop pushing against the wind and let yourself soar high."

"I don't understand, George."

"You will in time my dear Ava. As we float and soar, we experience the wondrous feeling within from the gentle touch of someone who cares, and the joy when we accomplish something we've worked hard for."

"Like finding my father!"

George's eyes sparkled with his love.

"Yes, my Lady, and bringing him home."

The precious moment was moment was interrupted by Morgan, cursing loudly. "Gone!" was what he meant.

"MORGAN! Watch your language," Ellie chastised him.

"Well, it is gone. Run like a coward! Come and fight me if you think you're hard enough," he shouted, turning back to the space that had held the black swirling mass of Nothingness."

"All in good time master Morgan."

"What's that?" Tarran shouted.

They looked where he was pointing, upwards. Two gigantic white wings were seen flapping with such power that clouds dissolved as it swept by.

"The swan?"

"No, it's the wrong shape to be the swan or the Queen," answered Lexi.

The giant bird came clearly into view as it landed near George and Ava. George knew immediately who it was and stood up instantly and bowed.

"Your Majesty," he said.

The giant white crane hovered above the ground, gradually transforming into the King.

"Commander George, Winifred, ladies, gentlemen," he said with a courteous bow of his fairy head. "Ava, my dear," he whispered as he raised his hand to help Ava up.

"Hello, your majesty," she replied, straightening her T-shirt and shorts.

"Your powers are growing, my Lady. The

transformation into a dragonfly is quite remarkable, especially one so regal with royal blue wings. I must say, the wife and I were most impressed, what-what."

"Pardon your Majesty? You saw that?"

"We see everything. We are Fae and we are everywhere, or almost so. I hear you made the acquaintance of King Samphire. In the battle ahead he will be useful."

"Sire, if you saw me, why didn't you help me free my father?"

"Because we simply do not have that much power yet. When you have collected at least half of the treasures, that's when our strength shall return, and we can become a fighting force, but all in good time. Now, that brings me to the reason I am here, what-what."

The aunts gathered round the King, as did they all. Only Tarran remained somewhat distant. He was studying the fairy King and had a better view further back.

"I can verify that the treasure you must now find is indeed the sword of Rhyddech the Generous which was forged in the Age of Dragon. It was known to us as the Flaming Sword or White Hilt. It always belonged in our world but found its way into yours through King Arthur."

Tarran practically jumped forward towards the King.

"Did you say Arthur, sir? As in the Sword in the Stone?"

"The very same, Master Tarran."

"But that was a myth!"

"All myths have some element of truth at heart, what-what."

Tarran was silenced, Morgan was silenced, Winifred

was silenced as was Ellie and Lexi for they knew how personal this quest was going to be for Ava. Winifred worried for her niece on this journey. When the King spoke of Arthur, Winifred winced as if she had been pierced by the sword itself. This quest would bring Ava into direct contact with her mother. Winifred closed her eyes as Lexi placed her hand on Winnie's shoulders for support.

"Now ladies and gents, hear these words:

Dancing dragons entwined in stone,
Swiftly soar through air and foam,
Forever immortalised in gold,
A knight's tale told from passages of old."

"I can't remember that," said Ava.

"It is written in your corens."

"Corens?" she asked.

"Books," said Tarran.

"Well done, Master Tarran. You'll be a scholar of Fae in no time. We are always in need of a good ambassador, aren't we Commander Wrenn, what-what?"

"Indeed, your Majesty."

"Well, I should be on my way. Good day, my lady. Bif-bang ladies and gents. Commander Wrenn, keep up the good work, what-what."

"Sir," George saluted back and clicked his heels together as he bowed to the King who had morphed once more into the giant white crane. He took one leap into the air and his mighty wings carried him further and further until he was out of sight.

"Excellent!" said Winnie. "Now we know we are on the right track and what to look for."

"Aye, the sword Brenna. Will it be in the book do you think, Winnie?"

"Can't do harm to look, can it. Let's go, ladies and gents." Aunt Winifred curled her arm around Ava. "Come along darling, as soon as we find that sword, the sooner your father will be home with us."

Ava's heart felt heavy as lead while she trudged back to the house.

Turning around, she bowed her head to General Ignatius.

"Thank you," she said to him, softly.

He saluted her. His army flying behind him in rows of dragonflies also saluted Ava as she walked back to the house. Aunts Holly, April, Guinevere and Eowyn had taken to the twilight sky to do a perimeter sweep of the grounds, one going east, one going west, one south and one north. It was a dance they had performed many times before. The four witches gracefully glided through the summer night sky on their brooms, searching keenly for any sign of the enemy.

6. The Lady Aethelflaed

"You'll never guess what we found in the magic room, Ava," Morgan said as they entered the library.

Books were strewn across the floor along with chocolate wrappers and plates of biscuits. Morgan held up a leather seat. It was too big for a horse, too oblong for an elephant and just not the right shape for any kind of normal riding.

"Now then, where did we get up to? Ava be a dear and check The Book for me please for the King's dragon quote."

The Book was the family grimoire that Ava had begun to study. Tarran loved reading it to. They spoke the spells and incantations, listed the mysterious ingredients and gawped at the unrecognizable creatures drawn into the margins. Ava ran her hand over the book. She felt a tingle of electricity shoot up her fingers as they travelled over the leather-bound pages, grazing the margins. The feeling ran up her arm, all through her body, making her hair stick up.

Commander Wrenn said, "Energy. It manifests itself in different forms. It never dies, it merely transforms. The transformation of energy is universal, for all things are connected. The power or energy flows through you Ava, just as time does. That is why you were able to become a dragonfly."

Aunt Winifred fidgeted in her chair.

"Yes, yes, George, now come on people, let's get to work. Ava, The Book if you please. Thirteen Treasures. Anything to do with dragons. Thank you."

"Right," said Ava, turning the pages, searching for the

Thirteen Treasures.

"Tarran, Morgan search those historical books on dragons please," said Aunt Winifred. "Brenna and Fawn, the flipchart. Lexi, another batch of coffee if you please. Something tells me we are in for a long night."

The aunts scurried off to complete their designated tasks as Tarran and Morgan searched books on dragons. Morgan had decided to sit on the leather seat with its huge, long straps sprawled out on the floor. They seemed to stretch out for ever like an octopus' legs and had buckles at the end intended to tie onto something.

"Is that thing comfortable?" Tarran asked.

"Aye, perfectly you jarring, urchin-snouted starveling," Morgan answered indignantly. Their rivalry had turned into a playful battle of wits which occasionally transcended into insults straight from Shakespeare.

Fawn and Brenna brought the flipchart in and placed it in front of them. Ellie moved the coffee table out of the way.

"Ooh, isn't this all positively exciting, Winnie?" said Fawn. "To think that we are about to become part of The Awakening."

"I don't know about you Fawn," said Meadow, curtly, "but we've been awake for some time, just didn't think the final battle would happen in our lifetime, let alone our children's."

"Come on now ladies, let's get to it politely, please," said Ellie, sensing Winnie's anxiety for her niece.

"There's nothing here auntie, just the same stuff we've read about before. It repeats what the Thirteen Treasures are."

"Mmm, okay. Anything about the sword?"

"Only stuff we've read before," Ava said, running her fingers over the page. She felt something on her fingertips. Looking down to the bottom of the page, she noticed a small, faded pink rose which seemed to be embossed within underneath the list of The Thirteen Treasures. "That's odd."

"What is dear?" asked Winifred.

"This pink rose appeared from nowhere. It wasn't there before, I'm sure of it. It's a wild rose," Ava added as they all leaned over to see what she meant.

An expression of understanding passed between them, one after the other until all of them realised what it was they were seeing. The aunts then said in unison.

"Briar Rose!"

"Aethelflaed," Aunt Winfred said before adding, "Lexi check the…"

Before Winifred had the chance to finish the sentence, Aunt Lexi was already running to the history section of the library.

"On it Winnie," Lexi replied with her hands waving in the air.

At the same moment, Morgan raised his hand excitedly, pointing to something in the book he was holding.

"Here, here it is," he shouted, and he read aloud:

Legends of the Dragons: In the year of our great Lord Alfred, a daughter of grace was born to him. Her name Aethelflaed meaning 'noble beauty' derives from the time of her birth in the month of May when the wild roses bloom. She is the Briar Rose of history and was definitely a thorn in the side of the Vikings.

She became known as the Lady of Mercia and was a fearless warrior and commanding leader. Legend says that her sword helped forge one of the mightiest and most mystical swords ever, The White Hilt.

"Great! Excellent! Where is it? And where's Mercia?"

As always, Professor Tarran had all the answers.

"Basically, the Midlands. It was one of the Seven Kingdoms of England - Northumbria, Mercia, East Anglia, Essex, Kent, Sussex and Wessex."

"Right, so the sword could be in Lincoln then?"

"Hold on there, Ava," said George. "We need to understand the quote. It's one thing to understand what the sword is made of, it's another to find it." George held his hand in the air, telling them to listen. "We need to find the meaning of the sword, but most of all we need to find the origin of his majesty's quote. Try the book, Legends of the Vitrified Forts. Mistress Winifred, do you have a copy of that?"

"I believe I do, Commander Wrenn. Check the shelf on dragons. At the top. That's it."

"Excellent. Thank you."

"You might need the lad…"

Aunt Winifred was about to say ladders but realised top shelves were not a problem for a Fae commander.

George floated along, touching each spine with the tip

of his finger, until…

"Aha! Here it is!"

He pulled out a huge book and blew on it, scattering dust everywhere as he drifted back down to the ground.

Tarran, still lost in his own discoveries, called out excitedly,

"Oh! Listen to this:

The House Seton with the green dragon emblem on its crest were highly acclaimed dragon riders. Their prowess for riding and training dragons was second to none and their natural strength and freedom combined with dragons' fire ensured that the House Seton was a formidable enemy on the battlefield.'

"You know what this means, Morgan? You're a natural dragon rider."

Morgan's eyes lit up as Tarran showed him a picture of a Seton family member riding a dragon which might well have been Samphire. Turning the page, they saw a range of odd shapes.

"Look Morgan! It's the seat you're sitting on! It's a special saddle for riding a dragon."

"Wow!" Morgan turned to Ellie. "Look Ma," he said pointing at the picture, "can I learn to do such a thing? Me?"

"No, you most certainly cannot," Aunt Ellie firmly said. "If you can't ride a motorbike, you are most definitely not going to ride a dragon."

"Oh, Ma!"

"No, Morgan."

"But Ma!"

"That's final. No motorbike and no dragon," and with that Aunt Ellie crossed her arms.

"Well, actually Auntie Ellie," Tarran rather meekly added, "Morgan could in theory apply for his provisional licence."

Aunt Meadow leaned close to Tarran and whispered conspiratorially in his ear.

"Not helping sweetie," and she shook her head, sadly, adding, even more quietly, "Patience, patience, dear boy."

7. The Dark Fae and The Wolf

The library fell silent as heads turned to books, but the words on the page remained unread as everyone had been distracted by a mother and son argument. Brenna looked at Winifred who rolled her eyes in frustration.

This was only the two boys. What would it be like when they all arrived? Wolfe, Marsden and Bram - the Welsh Trinity as Tarran called them. The final 'cousin', as Ava thought of them, was Chay, the son of Jissika Artasak. Although he lived on the Scottish Island of Skye with his mother, he followed his mother's Inuit ways.

Ava thought he was most mysterious. He had a quiet presence about him and loved nothing better than to be out in nature roaming free, living in tents, hunting and eating from the land. It felt like such a long time since she had seen Chay. Out of all the aunts, Jissika Artasak was the one that hardly ever ventured south. She loved the cold, so when it was Yule and Imbolc she would come to stay, and Chay would often join her.

Jennifer loved Chay too; all animals seemed to love Chay. He had such a presence, everything just wanted to be near him. Aunt Jissika knew what he was when he was born, she knew his destiny.

"He's going to be a great medicine man," she had said proudly one snowy Samhain. She had come down on the rare occasion to the family for New Year, as even in October she felt it too warm in Candlesby Manor.

The Welsh Trinity were different again. Marsden and Wolfe were rough and tumble type of boys who Ava couldn't understand whilst Bram was her favourite of the three. Right from an early age he wanted to get dressed up in different costumes. When Aunts Fawn and Brenna got married a couple of years before, Ava was their flower girl, only she didn't want to wear the dress, Bram wanted to wear it. And so he did. Although Ava was the official flower girl, it was Bram who wore her dress as Ava walked down the aisle scattering flowers in her cut off worn jean shorts and T-shirt.

The four aunts who had been completing flying perimeter checks came in.

"That's that shift done," said Aunt Holly while placing her broomstick back in the closet next to the library. Aunts Guinevere, Eowyn and April followed suit.

"Right, next shift starts," replied Fawn putting the flipchart pen lid back on as she and Aunt Brenna had been writing intermittent notes on the chart as the information had been discovered. On the board was written:

Aethflaed

Dragon-rider

Briar Rose

House Seton

"That far eh?" Eowyn said as she passed the flipchart.

"Mmm, aye, slow going. You guys might have better luck with it," replied Brenna.

Aunt Fawn was already at the closet getting their brooms prepared.

"What's going on here, then?" April asked.

"Looking for the sword quote, Aethflaed and dragons, Aunt April."

"So, the usual stuff then?"

"Yep," replied Ava, turning the page to navy blue coloured page with white writing. "Auntie, what's the Dark Fae? And have you ever seen it?"

Aunt Winifred's eyes tightened as the others pretended to ignore the question.

"A long time ago Ava, when I was just a little older than you, I changed for the first time."

The diamond shape had appeared on Ava's forehead once more.

"Changed into what Auntie, a witch?"

"A wolf."

Tarran's eyes widened.

"A wolf?"

"Do you remember that Ellie?"

"Oh yes. It was an amazing sight to behold."

"Indeed, it was, Mistress Winifred. The enemy didn't know where to hide," said George.

Ava, Tarran and Morgan closed their books as they anxiously waited for Aunt Winifred to tell her story. She slowly took off the glasses that perched on the end of her nose.

"It was just after the clocktower had been destroyed and before my mother, your grandmother Ava, had the new one built. Your father was away at school with your Morgan's father, up in Scotland.

"We had always heard the stories about a werewolf in our family of witches but it had been so long since any one had been born into the family that we thought the wolf bloodline had been bred out. You see only the threat of the Dark Fae can entice the wolf out of its slumber."

"What happened?"

"I went out to pick some wild blueberry one evening, out on the southside just before you reach the wych elms. It's funny, I always preferred the night and I always loved a full moon," Winifred reminisced.

"Auntie?"

"Oh yes, well, I was minding my own business when, without wawrning, this dark energy surrounded me. It was a presence like I had never experienced before. The world grew darker than night and I felt something so evil all around. The most frightening creatures swarmed towards me with grey faces and deep red eyes. They were hideous, small as a fairy but intent on doing me great harm.

"They chanted something and started scratching and cutting my arms and legs - but without ever touching me. I had to get home, but it was so dark I couldn't find my way. I mean it was night, but it was a thick, impenetrable blackness, except for their evil red eyes.

"I stumbled and fell along the path and wished for the moon or some starlight to find me. Blood was dripping down my arms and legs as I ran along in madly in the darkness, those hideous creatures chasing close behind.

And then I saw it. Lady Anne's Lace stood tall and paved the way out of the darkness. A shaft of light radiated from it, illuminating the path for me with a glow of divine grace. Something, some instinct I think, prompted me to eat one of its flowers - and I did.

"As soon as it touched my lips, my legs gave way and I fell to the ground whereupon I watched my hands turn to paws! I tried to yell but instead a howl came out. The full moon appeared from behind a cloud - and I don't remember much after that."

Everyone was silent. The library was still until Ava asked.

"Does it happen every full moon?"

"No, I used to change only when the Dark Fae were near, but now I have learnt how to control it. I will readily admit, sometimes it does take me off guard and the transformation will happen without warning."

"What are the Dark Fae? Are they a part of the Nothingness?"

"No, the Dark Fae are their own entity, they are the Hollow, the fae of changelings, switching children with their own evil kind. They are drawn to those who have their own power or children who will one day grow up to do great things. These are the children they like to swap for a changeling fae child. They have been around for as long as time itself.

"Remember Ava," said Aunt Guinevere, "this is a world of duality. We are dictated to by the environment, by our place in the universe. We have sun and moon, day and night, summer and winter, and ultimately we have good and bad, and that includes everything even magic. When we do not live in harmony with nature, the human world and our world becomes a dangerous place.

"But the Dark Fae are no friends to humans; they hate and despise us. They have tried many times to destroy us and in centuries past they almost succeeded."

Aunt Eowyn continued the story.

"The witch hunts of the 16th and 17th centuries were partly their doing and a great many of our sisters and brothers were killed."

"But wicked witches existed though, right?" Tarran asked.

"Yes, son," Ellie replied, "but we take care of our own. There was no need for them to be killed and tortured in such a way. The Fae themselves could see what was happening so a great battle was fought, the Battle of the Poppies. Commander Wrenn led the Royal troops alongside the King against the Dark Fae."

George had changed into a 1920's Ivy League freshman complete with a pastel pink fairisle tank top over cream shirt and grey slacks. He continued,

"Many fae on both sides were killed. It is often said that the blood and misery that poured into the earth during that fateful battle sowed the seeds for the Nothingness, an entity so powered by destruction, death and sorrow at its core that only the Celtic Messiah himself can destroy it."

The library grew quiet again. Ava tried to focus on researching where the next treasure might be found, but the enormity of her task had quenched her understanding and she found herself re-reading the same sentence over and over again.

She slammed the Book shut and let out a huge sigh of frustration and asked her aunt,

"When is Bram coming, Aunt Eowyn?"

"He is with his father and Marsden and Wolfe. They've all gone on a camping holiday in Snowdonia for July, but they'll be here for Lammas. Why? Do you miss Bram? He's grown so big he won't fit into any of your clothes now."

A shout from George interrupted them.

"Yes! Here it is! I knew it would be in this book. I just knew it! Me oh my!"

When George got excited about something, he sparkled more, especially when he was in human form.

"April, Guinevere, write this down will you please.

Dancing dragons entwined in stone,
Swiftly soar through air and foam,
Forever immortalised in gold,
A knight's tale from passage of old.

"This passage was found engraved on one of the vitrified forts in Dun Deardail in Glen Nevis which stems from 500 BC."

"Vitrified forts?"

"Vitrification is when rock is heated to such a degree that it turns to glass."

"Is that the Castle of Glass?"

"It may well be Ava, but we have yet to find twelve more treasure before the castle appears to us. I think this is our first real clue. We need to go to Scotland and Dun Deardail, my Lady Winifred."

"Wait a minute, wait a minute." Tarran waved his hands in the air. "Vitrification in 500 BC? Where could they find anything that powerful to melt rock so that it turned to glass? I mean, they didn't have lasers back then, so how were the vitrified forts made?"

"Dragons, master Tarran!" George replied. "They made the vitrified forts of Aberdeen. Remember, they were often friends to man and a great many noble houses had them." George spoke to Tarran but was staring at Morgan who beamed at the prospect of one day riding a dragon.

"Right," said Winnie, "there's not a moment to lose. Let's get a good night's sleep and be up with the dawn to head to Scotland. Ellie and Morgan, you're with us on this one. Holly stay behind and organise Lammas this year please with Lexi. Tarran and Meadow you are also required as is Chay and Jissika. April, could you be a love and fly on up to Lewis and request them to meet us three days from now on Castle Island at Loch Leven?"

"Yes Winnie, right away. Should I return or stay with them?"

"Stay please, April. We will need all hands, methinks. And I have a feeling we will need the power of the Welsh for this."

"Absolutely Winnie, I shall leave immediately. See you soon Ava. I shall let Meadow and Lexi know what's going on," and with that, April grabbed her broomstick from the hall cupboard and set off.

"I will make some fresh hot chocolate for us all and then it's off to bed for you three," fussed aunt Holly, taking the tray from the library.

"When do the boys arrive, Guinevere?"

" The thirtieth of July, Winnie."

"Mmmm, that's a bit too late. Could they make it the twenty-fifth?"

"I will let Osian know."

Osian was the father of Bram and was the one of only two men that had 'survived' being connected to the Thirteen. The other was Tarran's father. The mysterious deaths, break ups and eventual divorces that ensued was just a small price to pay for being connected to such powerful women.

Ava noticed Aunt Winifred anxiously fidgeting with her hands and fingers.

"Are you alright, auntie?"

"Yes dear. I'm wondering how to get up there - to Scotland."

"Motorbike?" Tarran suggested.

"Dragon?" Added Morgan winking at Tarran.

Aunt Winifred had a smile of mischief and mystery, and with her long snow-white hair, when she caught you with that look of hers, appeared as if she belonged in fairy tale.

"I think it's time you children experienced the power of this world, the power of nature and of light. Be up for dawn tomorrow children."

"Beddy-byes, the lot of you," said Aunt Ellie, and with that she ushered the young ones to their bedrooms… just as

Holly came out with the hot chocolate.

"Perfect timing, Holls," she said as she handed each of them their drink, then told them,

"Off you go now. Dawn and danger will soon be upon us."

8. The Path

Tread the single path – from out of the dark step into the light.

Ava lay awake in bed, staring at the ceiling. The shadows of flying witches doing their perimeter checks of the grounds would occasionally drift round her room as they flew past her window. What on earth was travelling by nature going to entail?

She had already travelled by cloud, and she had changed into a dragonfly. What else could happen? Ava shook her head as she tossed and turned.

"Got to find that second treasure. Got to find that sword," she mumbled into the pillow. She felt her eyelids grow heavy and she drifted off for only a moment when she was awakened by George.

"Come along, come along. Dawn is nearly upon us. Downstairs in ten minutes please, Princess Ava. Chop-chop."

Ava rubbed her eyes.

"But it's still dark out."

"Well, aren't we the perceptive one? Yes of course it's still dark. We need the first beams of dawn to travel. Now hurry up, Ava, get to it," and with that, George was gone.

Ava could hear a great amount of clattering going on downstairs as she ventured into the kitchen adjusting her backpack straps. All she had was her father's journal, a spare set of clothes and a pencil. Aunt Winifred noticed Ava first.

"Darling, there you are. All ready, are we? You don't need much. You've got everything you ever need right here," and she pointed to Ava's heart and winked.

Morgan and Tarran were checking each other's back packs. Tarran had packed books whereas Morgan on the other hand had a never ending supply of chocolate, crisps, drinks and a random selection of sweets such as jelly babies and jelly beans, which he viewed as one of his five-a-day fruits.

Aunts Ellie and Meadow were checking their bags. Meadow made sure she had the first aid kit whereas Ellie had the witch's travel kit, consisting of blue moon salt, magic water, a selection of herbs such as basil, mint, sage, lavender and thyme and finally an array of leaves and bark from various trees around the estate, including Grandmother Apple's bark for healing and Grandfather Oak's acorns for protection, numerous hawthorn leaves, not to mention a handful of sister wych elms' leaves for their explosive fighting power. It was a travel kit of rare riches.

"Excellent. Are we already then? Good, let's go. Lexi, we will be back in time for Lammas. Continue making everything ready, please."

"Of course, Winnie. Keep safe."

Aunt Winifred ushered everyone else out into a dark summer's night. The smell of the air was cool, yet tinged with something else, a potion of power, heat and a spark of electricity, mixed generously with excitement.

The seven made their way towards the Heart of the

Forest and the stone circle. The trees creaked and rustled their leaves as witches and children walked silently through the night to the clearing where the stone circle lay.

"Right everyone, stand in the circle and hold hands. We are just in time. George are you…"

"Yes, my lady."

George transformed himself into the commanding fae that he was, complete with blue-white wings and General's uniform.

"Get ready, Ava," said Aunt Meadow.

Ava glanced round at the circle of family and friends holding hands. Morgan was beaming with his expectations of an adventure whilst Tarran was his usual calm self, albeit with a slightly apprehensive expression.

Through the tree, shooting down from the sky, came the first beams of light chasing the black of night away.

"Now children," said Winfred, "believe. Believe in the power of light inside you. Imagine a glowing flame within connecting you to the light of day without. Join the light and become one."

Ava was about to ask her how, what and why - when she noticed a beam of light touch the tips of her fingers. They tingled and, as she watched, the dawn's light stretched further up her hand. As the beam grew stronger her fingers slowly faded, then her hand, wrist and arm shimmered and vanished in a sparkling dance of swirling tiny bubbles of light.

Ellie and Meadow were almost completely gone. Tarran had his eyes closed but he too faded as the first beam of light grew stronger and spread further into the circle of seven. Morgan was shimmering but he could see that Ava was still holding on to the dark.

"Believe in yourself Ava. Picture that glowing spark inside of you connecting to the dawn's light."

Morgan called to her, but his voice lingered longer than he did, for as he shouted out her name, he too disappeared along with Tarran, Ellie and Meadow.

Aunt Winifred opened her eyes.

"Ava, let go darling and believe. You especially can do this."

With the final burst of the dawn's early light, the beam finished its journey. Aunt Winifred too vanished into the light leaving Ava standing alone in the misty early morning.

Ava stood bereft and scared in the stone circle.

'What do I do now?' she asked herself, but no answers came, only silence. She fell to her knees and could feel tears burning down her cheeks. So many thoughts and images raced through her head, but the main one was, 'I am no good. I am a failure. I cannot complete this task.'

"I'm no good," she cried into her hands.

A soft warmth permeated through her from a gentle hand on her shoulder.

"If only you could see what I see when I look at you, Ava."

George in human form stood over her. The compassion in his eyes stopped Ava's tears.

"I thought you'd gone with the others."

"My dear girl, I can never leave you. Remember the

king's order. Not that I would ever leave you anyway. You are a child of Fae and I could never disobey your mother."

"You know my mother?"

"Of course, we all do. Some of us have even met her Ava. You should meet her one day. You remind me a lot of her. And because of her you have so much power inside you, if only you could believe in yourself.

"Look at all you have accomplished so far, my dear. You are not just a girl, you are a wonder. And you need to start believing. Now, come on take my hand and let's catch up wirth the others."

"But how? The dawn light has ended."

George said, "You know, you are beginning to sound more like a witch everyday, my dear. There are more ways to travel than on a sunbeam. You of all should know that. Plus, have you forgotten who you are with? I am an officer of the Fae, a commanding general.

"Come along and meet Grandfather Oak. You haven't met him yet, have you?"

"No, but Grandfather Oak? You mean that giant tree in the centre of the grounds?"

"The very same."

Ava picked herself up off the ground and brushed the dirt away.

"How?"

"You'll see. Follow me."

George marched on towards the giant oak tree which stood as if to attention, having watched all the comings and goings of the family Fellow for centuries.

Approaching the tree, it creaked and groaned and looked to all intents and purposes alive. The crinkled, wrinkled bark shimmered and a face appeared.

"Well well, young Master Wren, and the little sprite herself. Good morning my lady Ava. Miss the sunbeam, did we? Never fear, my dear girl, use my stair way and venture through the axis mundi of the world."

Ava looked at the wise face in puzzlement.

"The axis mundi?"

George came to the rescue.

"The axis mundi, Ava - Grandfather Oak's roots venture deep underground and connects the worlds beneath whilst his branches connect the lands above."

Ava tried to picture this beautiful image which filled her with wonder and hope.

"Follow the stairs to the world where your aunt is waiting. Three steps should do it."

The tree trunk twisted round further and opened like a space capsule.

Ava peered inside.

The doorway was small, though perfectly adequate for her and George to get through. She searched the darkness.

"George, are we meant to go in there?" she asked, as she pointed to the silent black hole hidden within a talking tree!

"Yes, of course we are. Off we go. Thank you, Grandfather Oak. As always, you've come to the rescue." George ventured into the trunk, patting it as he did so.

The tree chuckled as it turn its trunk around, closing the doorway.

George did not hear the answer, but Grandfather Oak was used to being alone.

"Of course, I am an oak tree after all, and from small acorns do we mighty oaks grow. How stupendous is that!"

The trunk door sealed shut.

9. The Forest

As soon as the trunk had closed like a great cathedral door, Ava blinked a couple of times to allow her eyes to grow accustomed to the dark. She needn't have done so for no sooner had the trunk closed than a thousand tiny lights shone on the walls, on the steps and the handrail. All around her was wood, not just oak but the wood of every tree and plant found in the forest.

The handrail was made from wild rosewood whilst rambling roses twisted down into the darkness of a never-ending staircase sequenced with three kinds of wood - one step was dark walnut, another was mahogany and the next an almost white poplar. The walls glowed luminescent with ash and maple.

Ava took a deep breath, the smell of wood permeating her nostrils. She was expecting it to be dark, damp and fusty in a tree trunk, but instead it was light, warm and sweet. The little lights graced not only the walls but steps too as the spindles of the bannister. They seemed to dance and sparkle intermittently weaving around the bannister and handrail's carvings of roses and leaves.

"What are they, Goerge? Fairies?"

George replied with an indignant harrumph!

"No, they are most certainly not fairies! They are lichens blessed by the Goddess herself. They live here permanently and light the way for all weary travellers, day and night, who need to pass through the Axis Mundi of the world, as souls sometimes need to do. Now remember what

Grandfather Oak said, three steps should do it."

"I don't know how that's going to work."

George raised one eyebrow again.

"Faith, Ava. Please believe."

"Alright, alright. One…"

Ava counted as she moved on to the first step.

As she did so, the whole tree trunk shifted and the lichens changed colour from white to blue. As she stepped onto the next one, they changed to an almost incandescent cyan. In the distance she could hear the crying and screeching of seagulls.

A door formed on the ash and maple walls, a door in knotted pine.

When she made the final step, the door was before her.

"Scot's pine," George remarked, "how appropriate. Turn the handle will you please Ava, as much as it's lovely here, let's go, shall we?"

Ava took one last look around.

She leaned over the handrail and gazed down into the blackness. She could see a gigantic forest forming from each step. It was the forest of the world mirrored beneath the ground, a world within worlds.

"What's down there, George?" she asked.

"The other side of the other side," he answered, enigmatically. "Each step leads to another world, I believe."

"How can you tell where you are going?"

"Good question, but the rule is - odd numbers take you to places on Earth, whereas even numbers take you, well, elsewhere. But never take twenty-two steps, Ava, never."

"Why?"

"Because that will take you to heaven, and that's somewhere I cannot go, and for that matter, neither can you."

Ava was shocked.

"I can never go to heaven?"

"It's not that you can't go, my princess, it's just that we don't go there, like humans. We go somewhere else."

"Where?"

"The Summerlands, Ava. Shall we discuss this later? Now come on, we should press on."

Ava was quietly expectant as she reached out her hand to the ebony door in the tree trunk. She didn't even think about what could be on the other side after what George had just said. She always thought she would go to heaven, but then again, Summerlands did sound appealing.

She shrugged her shoulders, tilted her head and curled her fingers around the door handle, gave a little nudge and pushed.

A beam of light stretched its way into the tree. The lichens dwindled back into the steps and bannisters once more as if to hide from the light of the human world.

Ava stepped out into the day and breathed the air. It was so much cooler and fresher. She looked up to the sky and saw the seagulls as they squawked at each other. She knew where she was - Scotland. She glanced round as George stepped behind her, closing the door of another giant oak tree. The trunk twisted around, hiding its secret world.

"Trees are the gatekeepers of sacred doorways," said

George, "in which time and space are shaped. We must keep their knowledge and presence safe in this world. Think how much of your own Amazonian rainforest has been destroyed. How many ancient doorways and portals have been lost forever, worlds we can no longer travel to?"

George shook his head in dismay at the wanton destruction wrought by humanity. Ava placed her hand on his shoulder.

"All will be well once we have found the final treasure, George, and the Celtic Messiah returns. We can grow new forests for a new age."

George patted Ava's hand.

"Absolutely, absolutely Ava. What a special girl you are. Now then, let's catch up with the others, shall we?"

10. Out of The Dark and Into the Light

Ava and George walked silently side by side and emerged out of the forest onto a craggy landscape. In the distance Ava could see silhouettes of people and one in particular came into view, Morgan. Ava waved, Morgan waved back and then ran towards her.

The cobbled stones on the path gleamed with a dew that also made them slippery. As Ava quickened her pace towards Morgan, she slipped. George grabbed her arm.

"Careful Ava the vitrified stones can be quite treacherous when damp."

"They are like glass, George."

"Precisely. Rock exposed to such a high temperatures, they have indeed turned to glass."

Morgan reached them, excited and keen to talk.

"Isn't it something, Ava? Come and see what we've found."

"The treasure?"

"Er, no. Something interesting, though, a rock with my family's crest scorched into it. Come on."

He shouted and waved, running back to the others, slipping and sliding as he went.

By the time Ava and George had caught up to them, Tarran and Aunt Meadow were trying to dig the rock out of the wall. Aunt Winifred gave Ava a huge hug.

"Oh, darling, well done. Grandfather Oak?" she asked George, who tilted his head slightly, upon which Ellie stepped forward to give Ava a cuddle.

"Mon Cherie. I knew you would find your way."

Tarran looked up from trying to pull the rock out.

"Never doubted it for a moment, Ava."

"Where are we exactly, auntie?"

"Dun Deardil, my dear. The vitrified hillfort built about 2500 years ago, so a bit before my time."

"And mine," said Ellie.

"That's Glen Nevis, and over there is Ben Nevis. And right, right over there is Castle Seton," Morgan excitedly pointed.

"Push it, Tarran, push it! Put some weight into it boy," Meadow commanded her son.

Ava, being very much a conservationist, objected.

"Why are you doing that?" she asked. "This is an archaeological site, you are not allowed to touch anything, let alone destroy a centuries old wall. Tarran I'm surprised at you," she scolded.

"We believe there's something deeper there," said Morgan, "something important. Plus, it will match the original one my ancestor took years ago that's now in the castle. Here Tarran, let me have a go."

Morgan took one giant kick at the wall, reminiscent of smashing the school's gates from which he had been expelled. The rock separated from its millennia old bed and bounced on the floor.

"Yes, I'm sure we are not meant to do that with archaeological sites, Morgan," said Aunt Winifred, "but it had to be done, and you did it well." Aunt Winifred glanced around, hoping that no one had seen them. "Commander

Wrenn, if we pool our powers together, could we not recreate the rock within the wall? No one would be the wiser."

"Yes, I think we can. We would need a small rock to replicate the one we've taken."

They hunted around for a few minutes until Ellie reappeared with a perfect specimen.

"Wonderful, Ellie. Right, gather round everyone, come close and with one hand on the broken wall and one on this rock say after me,"

> *Ancient guardian here I stand,*
> *With time and duty, I am bound.*
> *Build the wall upon these rocks,*
> *When I give three knocks.*

After they had all repeated the spell, the rock hovered in the air, unaided by human or fae hand. Tarran and Morgan stepped back from the crumpled wall as earth and chunks of masonry floated about. The hovering rock altered shape and colour until it was identical with the one they had taken.

"Look at that, just look at that! Not bad at all, is it?" Tarran whispered in admiration.

"Nevertheless, it was wrong."

"The wall looks as it did. No one will notice. And we have… this."

"What is it exactly?"

Ava reached out to touch the oval shape with its smooth corners and translucent golden and opal veins. She traced her fingers over the carved image of a dragon sprouting fire with its wings elevated with the words:

Prompta Tamen Periculum

Ava read the words out loud and translated it with Tarran both saying at the same time:

"Hazard, yet…"

"Forward!" shouted Morgan, jumping in between them. Ava and Tarran stared at him, shocked at the thought that he knew Latin.

"Well, I do know my family's motto, Mr and Little Miss Smarty Pants!"

Ava rolled her eyes and Tarran shook his head.

"Winnie," said Meadow, "what do you say we make our way to the castle for the night, try to fathom all this out."

Winifred agreed.

"Yes, indeed Meadow, we must. There is much to be discovered."

Ava glanced round, there wasn't a soul to be seen.

"Erm, auntie, how are we getting there?"

"How else, my dear, by bicycle and train."

Tarran's eyes narrowed, sweeping left to right while raising one eyebrow.

"We haven't brought our motorbikes."

"Aye, no motorbikes, quite right, but we are going on our bicycles, pedal power."

The aunts rummaged around in their rucksacks, pulling out tiny little model cycles, like something from a

Christmas cracker. Aunt Winifred placed hers on the ground, waved her hands gently and whispered an almost silent spell.

Zap!

A mint green bicycle appeared with a wicker shopping basket in the front and a bell on its handlebars. Aunt Meadow then did her magic bit by wafting her arms in the air saying, "Wishy-washy-woo, a bicycle made for two."

She clicked her fingers as Aunt Ellie sneezed and zap, in front of them appeared a tandem, complete with two neon pink seats. Ellie clapped her hands but Ava looked at them suspiciously.

"'*Wishy-washy-woo?*'"

Meadow and Ellie giggled.

"I always wanted to say it and it seemed the perfect opportunity."

"What about us?"

"Have you checked your rucksack, Morgan?"

"We didn't pack anything like that," answered Tarran, searching the rucksack on Morgan's back, digging deep into the endless sweet wrappers. His eyes suddenly lit up.

"Ooh, wait!"

His face screwed up as his hand emerged with a half-squashed jelly baby.

"Oh, that's where it is!" Morgan exclaimed as he pulled the sticky concoction off Tarran's finger and promptly plopped it in his mouth.

"Ew!"

"What are we going to ride?" Tarran asked his mother

whilst wiping his fingers.

"Oh, for heaven's sake Tarran, here!"

Aunt Meadow handed Tarran three tiny model bicycles.

Morgan and Ava leant forward peering into Tarran's hand.

"And what are we supposed to do with them?"

"Conjure yourselves up some bicycles, children. Go on Morgan. You are all capable. All of you have now seen enough to believe," Ellie said as, unladylike, she grappled to climb on the tandem with Meadow taking the front seat.

"Search inside yourselves for the right spell. Just start rhyming. Words have power, darling, when you make them your own."

The diamond formed on Ava's forehead again. George could see she wasn't impressed with the advice.

"Oh come, come Ava, and you as well Tarran and Master Morgan. All of you have energy and power within you. Tap into that and let's crack on, shall we?"

They stared at each other before Tarran shrugged his shoulders and said, "The power of words?"

"Aye, the power of words."

"The only master of words we know is Shakespeare, right?"

There were more famous modern authors, and Will was mainly just a name to most people, but the three of them had a little deeper knowledge than others.

"Let's brush up on it, then."

Tarran placed the tiny bicycles on the floor, took a deep breath and said, "When shall we three… ride again?"

"Upon these bikes we ride with them," said Ava.

"When the hurlyburly's done," added Morgan.

"When the battle's lost and won," said Ava.

Morgan waved his hands in the air like a demented magician before adding, "Skilly-scally-mah-mee, gift us our bicycles, one, two, three."

He clapped his hands with little hope and a flash of light momentarily blinded them. Their giggles stopped as they beheld three shiny mountain bikes lined up in front of them.

"No way!"

"Yes Tarran, way. Now come on children, let's cycle to the train station. George are you cycling or …"

"Flying, my Lady Winifred."

George clicked his fingers and switched immediately into his fairy form, the fairy Ava remembered from so long ago.

Aunt Winifred placed the prized rock in her shopping basket. "Let's go," she said.

In fits of giggles they cycled down the winding path towards the town. George flew close above Ava while Morgan led the way on his mountain bike.

They were so preoccupied, so intent on not falling off, that they failed to notice the white highland bobcat with purple tinged eyes staring at them the entire time.

"She's getting too powerful," thought the bobcat. "The Master will need to hear about this."

It sniffed the air and stretched and took on its true form. The long, sleek body of a certain Robin Goodfellow morphed into being, then vanished, leaving the grass where it had been sitting brown, withered and dead.

11. The Bridge

Cycling down to the train station was one thing; stopping was another as Ellie and Meadow found out as they disappeared into the station master's hedge.

In fits of laughter they emerged unscathed, brushing down their dresses and skirts as the station master came running to complain about his damaged hedge. He came to an abrupt stop and pointed.

"I thought you were riding bicycles and you'd lost control but there's nothing there. Where are they?"

Straightening her dress and glancing at the scene Aunt Ellie said, "No need to fuss. We lost our footing, sir, that's all. There's no bicycle and the hedge is healthily bouncy. I'm sure it will spring back up with a good rain shower."

The station master looked ready to explode as he stood staring at his flattened hedge.

"I say, excuse me, when is the next train to Torlundy please?"

Scratching his head and mumbling about seeing things, the poor man replied, almost in a robotic tone.

"The train on Platform 2, departing in five minutes."

"Excellent, excellent, thank you so much. Come along, come along everyone."

"But what about the bikes?" Tarran whispered to Winifred as she ushered everyone on to the platform, leaving the station master scratching his head while staring at the compressed hedge.

"We take them with us," George replied as he appeared

round the corner in a rather fetching tweed hunting jacket and knee length trousers with green and yellow tartan galoshes.

He clicked his fingers and the bicycles reverted to the their tiny sizes, sending Morgan ploughing into Ava, both of whom had been holding on to their precious cycles. They fell into each other and toppled over letting out little gasps of surprise and annoyance.

Scrambling to get up off Ava, Tarran and George held out their hands to help the two up as Morgan grabbed Tarran.

"We're lucky there was no-one around to see that," said Morgan. "All rather embarrassing, I'd say, and would need a fair amount of explaining away."

"Of course, I already knew there wasn't anyone around," said George, fibbing. "I checked the joint out," he winked, helping Ava up.

"Come on gang, there's the train, let's go," Meadow called out as she collected the miniaturised bicycles and shoved them in her bag.

The train was just one carriage and no-one else was getting on it. Tarran, Morgan and Ava sat at their table and aunts Winifred, Meadow and Ellie sat at theirs, opposite. George, of course, sat next to Ava as she nestled herself down close to the window. He was nothing if not attentive, and determined to protect his precious charge.

The only other people on the train were the driver and the conductor. The latter hurried out of the front cabin to sell tickets, then scurried back to the miniscule cabin afterwards, as if the passengers were something of a hindrance to his main duty - chatting to the driver.

Aunt Winifred had asked for one-way tickets, which made Ava shudder, as if a cold hand had brushed her back. One way, no need for a return.

Their journey was taking them further and further north. Although it was July, it was the north of Scotland and there was a chill in the air that seemed to permeate throughout the carriage.

Tarran got up and closed the window when he saw Ava tremble as Ellie fidgeted in her seat.

"Son, what sweets you got in that bag, then?"

"One of my five a day, Ma," Morgan replied, emptying his rucksack out on the table and rummaging through the empty sweet wrappers. He located a giant unopened bag of jellybeans.

"There you go, Ma, they'll keep you going," Morgan said, handing the bag to his mother.

"Just about."

The train lurched forward, chugging slowly out of the station. It picked up speed through the mountains and countryside as trees and heather zoomed past the window.

Tarran watched Morgan sort out his empty wrappers, desperately hunting for more sweets. He shared them round, but George screwed up his nose at them.

"Don't you eat thjem, George?"

"No, Master Morgan, fairies do not eat human food. We only eat flowers and occasionally leaves and only from plants that are in season in nature."

"Shame. You should try a jelly bean. What do you eat now, in July?"

"Well, that heather is looking rather scrumptious Master Morgan."

Beyond the window were rolling hills of heather and bracken. Beyond these were mountains and floating clouds of mist that seemed to be playing a game of catch with the train.

Ava hadn't been to Castle Seton for quite some time and neither for that matter had Morgan.

"When was the last time you were home, Morgan?"

"You mean the castle? I don't view it as home, never have. Me and Ma haven't spent that much time in it since Da, you know?"

Morgan's voice trailed off as he remembered his father.

Ava couldn't remember much about him, only that he seemed to be loud and jolly. He always made her father laugh with his antics and was always getting into trouble. A trait that Morgan had inherited, apparently, given the number of schools he had been expelled from.

Lord James Seton had been killed at sea when Morgan was only seven. Although he had never been found, a memorial for him was now on the castle's estate just by the side of the tiny chapel which also housed the tombs of the Setons.

After James had been killed, Ellie had left Castle Seton and drifted through various housing estates in Scotland hoping to find peace somewhere, and also hoping Morgan would remain in a school long enough to have an education.

"That's the fairy bridge at Glen Seton," Morgan pointed, fidgeting in his seat. He knew he was close to his ancestral home, even if he didn't acknowledge it as such.

"We're nearly there, Ma."

"I know, son."

"Do you think it's changed?"

"I doubt it. If it hasn't changed in a thousand years, it's hardly going to do so now."

Ellie shrugged her shoulders to Morgan as the others looked on, lost in their thoughts of all the battles and trials they had been through.

The single carriage train slowed down, taking forever to stop until it chugged its final breath into Torlundy station. Standing on the platform was April, smiling and waving. Aunt Winifred gave out a sigh of relief.

"Next part of the adventure, here we come."

She gathered up her belongings, taking especial care of the rock which she cradled in her arms like a baby.

"April, my dear, good to see you. All good?"

"Yes, yes, all good. Chay and Jissika are already making their way to Castle Island at Loch Leven, and I've brought the car."

"Excellent, April, thank you," said Ellie, mightily relieved, "I don't think I could do any more cycling for a while, at least not for another forty years."

"Come along then, the car is this way. I'm driving," April added shaking the keys.

"Will we all fit? We're a small army, you know, with a

fair amount of baggage."

The car was a bright metallic blue station wagon Range Rover with its spare tyre on the bonnet and three sets of seats and windows to match, plus benches at the back. It had bright white and yellow daisies painted on the doors.

"Say hello to Daisy," said Ellie.

Daisy looked like a big, beautiful monster but welcomed them all in, and their baggage, with a little wriggle room to spare. She was bouncy and galloped over the rough, rocky road to Castle Seton.

George sat on the bench behind Ava who sat in the middle with Tarran and Morgan on either side. The windy roads twisted and turned but Daisy carried on splashing through the creak as the clouds played catch up high above in the white dappled sky.

Daisy switched to mountain gear, roaring as she climbed a steep road up the cliff until turning to the right to reveal Castle Seton, nestled into the cliffs and rocks of a mountain that had its head in the clouds and its feet in the sea.

Castle Seton was a proper castle with turrets and a drawbridge. It had rising land and rolling hills to the side of it, complete with forests and a chapel, though a part of it had its dungeons in the sea.

Even though it looked desolate and alone, there was a warmth and a power emanating from it. It was hard to imagine the work needed to keep a place like that standing and in good order. Morgan was not the tidiest of boys, besides, he'd been away for a long period. The castle would not care for itself.

"Morgan," asked Ava, more aware of such concerns than Tarran, "who's been looking after the castle all this time?"

Morgan waited a while before replying.

"The staff," he answered, with a tinge of mystery.

Tarran and Ava glanced across at each other.

"Aye," he added, "Brownies."

12. The Quadruple Crossroads

One Path leads to Wales, one to Scotland, one to Ireland and one to England – Which one will you take?

As Daisy screeched to a stop, Tarran and Ava wondered nervously what would greet them inside. Morgan's answer had perplexed them, not that they didn't believe him, which of course they did. Morgan may have been a serial troublemaker at school, but he was never a liar.

It was the word Brownies. These were a rare highland species, independent and hard to pin down, not staff to care for an ancient edifice built into the side of a mountain.

Tarran and Ava had the utmost respect for fae. After all, Ava was known to be a child of Fae and in their service with the task of the Thirteen Treasures. Nevertheless, it was perplexing that Ellie and Morgan seemed to have casually left this glorious castle in the charge of Brownies. It was hard to imagine the truth of it.

The truth of it was even harder to imagine when they stepped out of the car and beheld the grounds.

The grass was cut perfectly, there were tidy flower beds, a couple of ponds, shrubs and trees, all lovingly cared for. Even the house, close up, was scrubbed and clean. It may have been ancient and in a windswept location, but was clearly maintained in surprising order. When they asked him again how all this was done when he and his mother did not live there for much of the time, Morgan repeated what he had already told them.

"Brownies, they do everything. Don't you believe me. You know I always tell the truth."

"Well, the windows are definitely shiny, look how clean they are Ellie. They're cleaner than mine," said Meadow, helping Ellie out the car.

"Yes, that would be Swann Merry of Thistle, she's in charge of glass and silver."

That was impressive. Not only did they have a staff of rare Brownies, but Ellie, and probably Morgan, too, knew who did what. Did each Brownie have a specific task? Were they that organised and attentive?

Ellie continued, "That's all windows, glasses, cutlery, and armour, not to mention pots and pans. She's quite excellent and equally sweet."

Winifred thought for a moment and said, "Isn't Bedwyr of Gales in your service, along with his brothers, Bleddyn Sky of Thorne and Berach Light of Whisper?"

Ava was growing more impressed by the moment. Not only did these Brownies care for the immense, ancient house, but they had immense, ancient names.

"Crickey Auntie, they're a mouthful, aren't they?"

Before Aunt Winifred could answer, George interrupted. He had been surveying the majestic site and had a quick fly around the grounds. He alighted on Daisy's trunk, deciding to educate his charges a little. He loved them and helped them and had faith in them, but sometimes they showed a woeful lack of knowledge.

"Brownies are of a noble Highland race. They are descended from the oldest and wisest Fae families and it is a true honour to have them working for you. In fact, they choose you, you can't employ them. Immensely proud elementals they are. Which reminds me, I should get dressed for the part."

He clicked his fingers and in a flash was dressed in his finest fairy uniform complete with commander's strips and medals.

His emerald green and white uniform was trimmed in gold brocade and his black boots came to his knees. His medals glistened in the light and his boots were so highly polished you could see your face in them.

"Now then, that's better. Shall we go in Master Morgan?"

Morgan gave an army salute and George saluted back, smoothing down the single crease in his silky jacket.

As the group approached the door it slowly creaked open, pushed or pulled by unseen hands.

Tarran and Ava were the first to peer round the door. They were not sure what to expect. This was a unique place in a unique spot, cared for in a unique way. Neither of them had ever seen Brownies before.

The others were only slightly less expectant. They followed the children in, relieved to be there, curious as to the reception they would be given.

Standing in a row facing the door were six of the cutest but oddest elemental Fae beings imaginable.

They had squashed faces that resembled a pug in many respects, and the biggest brown eyes like s soppy beagle puppy. They were incredibly cute but you couldn't call them lovely. Their expressions combined wisdom, fun, joy and industry. If you looked into their puddle brown eyes, you might sink into their ancient history for they were bottomless wells of light. Unless you love pugs, you would not call a pug beautiful, and in the same way, these creatures would not enter beauty contests, but they had their own inner beauty, and that shone through them, clearer than any superficial features.

And they were of course, brown, a deep, rich brown unlike the skin colour of any human or any animal the children had seen. Brown, after all, is not just brown. It comes in all shades, just as white people are never quite white. No, everything about them was unique. They could not be easily categorised, but above all, they emanated loyalty and demanded respect.

Ellie stepped forward first to greet them followed by Morgan.

Upon seeing Commander George Wren in his smart uniform, all the Brownies bowed at the same time. In fact, Ava noticed them all blinking at the same time, which was rather unnerving.

As Morgan followed his mother, the first one bowed to him with one hand across his chest and the other held aloft in a cavalier type of way.

"Master Morgan, it is an honour to have you home. We have kept the place spick and span, span and spick for you. May I also add how much you've grown."

"Thank you, Brynmar Astor of Lark. The gardens are looking wonderful."

A little giggle and squeal was heard from one of the other six.

"That would be my cousin, Florry Blush the Sweet. She's in charge of the gardens my Lord."

A little smile swept across the Brownie's face as she stepped forward, as if on parade. Her mouth went the full length of her face so her 'little' smile beamed from huge round ear to huge round ear.

They were dressed impeccably with not a ruffle or crease anywhere on their shirts or knee length trousers, and their brown shoes were highly polished. Florry Blush and Swann Merry wore pure white pinafore dresses over brown pantaloons etched with starched white lace at the ankles.

Everything was in order. There wasn't a speck of dust anywhere. Everything gleamed and was polished to within an inch of its life. Ava leant closer to Aunt Winifred and whispered, "Why don't we have a Brownie or two at Candlesby?"

"What are you saying about the manor Ava? Are you saying witches are untidy? Witches have more important things to do than clean," Winifred gave Ava a gentle nudge.

Stepping forward, Ellie said,

"Tell me Bedwyn of Gales, is the stone of Seton still in its place in the library? We need to research it… along with this."

Ellie pointed to the rock Winifred was cradling in her arms.

The Brownies all blinked at the same time as Bedwyn, a rather small Brownie compared to the others, answered.

"Yes, mistress, it's in the library in its rightful place."

Another rather serious one stepped forward. He gulped before speaking.

"Am I right in thinking then Ma'am, that you will be… making a mess?"

The witches looked at each other, trying to hide their merriment. Aunt Meadow raised her eyebrows and suppressed a little sigh.

"Yes, I'm afraid we will be making one hell of a mess."

The Brownies all clapped with happiness as they broke out in smiles and intermittent squeals of, 'Marvellous,' and 'Wonderful.'

"Further, Brynmar, we will be staying for a couple of nights."

They stopped clapping and their puppy eyes almost fell out of their rather large heads with excitement. The idea that they would have oodles of work to do for longer than they expected seemed to fill them with unending delight.

The next moment, literally in and with a flash, all but one vanished. Tarran did a double take.

"Where did they go?"

"To prepare your rooms."

The remaining Brownie blinked his eyes twice before he too disappeared.

"Morgan, show Ava where the library is please. Meadow do you want help me with dinner? I need to make the little helpers a honey cake as a thank you for taking care of the place for us."

"Honey cake?"

"Aye, Brownies love dairy and cakes."

"But I thought elementals didn't eat human food?"

"Only fairies are rather particular Master Tarran, whereas Brownies and other earth elementals are partial to certain human delicacies including bread, dairy and especially honey," George explained.

"Aye, come on now, to the library," Morgan said, leading the way.

As Ava entered the library, she knew, in a moment of unexpected recognition, that she had been there before.

It was a distant memory. She recalled sitting on her father's knee as Morgan played near his dad in front of a fire with a blue flame. Morgan was playing with the stone of Seton, which was now housed in a hexagonal glass cabinet, centre stage, within this magnificent library.

The library at Candlesby was something special, but Seton Castle library was different entirely.

It was floor to ceiling books with dragon decorated ladders that swung round the entire library. Even the furniture was upholstered book shelves. Around her were vast tomes, carved dragons, seats and tables with endlessly clever spaces for books.

Tarran's eyes lit up as he cautiously stepped into this heaven.

"Oh wow! Or should I say, O puer!" Tarran exclaimed while walking towards the wall of Latin volumes.

"Perhaps, oh boy?"

Morgan put his hand on Tarran's shoulder and pointed towards the stone.

Near the window was a huge desk with a leather chair. On the desk was a notebook with green embossed letters spelling 'Lord Seton'. In the inkwell stood to attention an iridescent pen.

"The Writstar of Draconia," George said.

"Writstar?"

"A writstar was someone who could write, and their writing tools also became known as a writstar. It is a fairy pen, or a writing implement from Fae, Ava. This one was made specifically for Lord Seton, Morgan's father in Draconia."

"Why is it so different to our pens?"

"It never runs out, and the ink is from the rainbow."

"What?".

"You'll see," said George.

In came Aunt Winifred still carrying the rock they'd found.

"Now then, where's this stone Morgan? Ah, there you are."

As Winifred approached the stone, the rock in her arms glowed. Flecks of cyan seemed to stream through it with gold. To all intents and purposes, it looked like a stunning chunk of lapis lazuli, but why would that be buried in a wall from thousands of years ago?

"Now then, just look at this, George. What do you make of it?"

"I have no idea, mistress. Perhaps we should take the lid off the cabinet and put them both together?"

"Be careful, Winnie," April added, looking rather

apprehensively at the glowing rock in Winifred's arms.

"Surely it can't do any harm. Go on Morgan, do the honours."

Winifred gestured to Morgan, encouraging him as he cautiously removed the top of the cabinet. Winifred moved closer to the stone and it too glistened with flecks of silver and turquoise.

"Try moving it away auntie, see what happens."

They stood back and watched Winifred slowly move the rock away. The streaming colours faded as did the Stone of Seton. The further Winifred moved away from the stone, the more it looked like a normal piece of rock. When she approached, once again the two rocks glowed and glistened with silver and gold flecks.

"What are they?"

"Do you think it's the sword?"

"No Ava, the sword is bigger, but they are something to do with... something!"

Aunt Winifred was stumped as she finished her dance with the rock, still cradled in her arms.

Finally, she placed the rock next to the stone, so close they were almost touching.

They stood back, watching the intermittent colours swirl round inside the rocks until the flecks of gold and silver flowed into one another, merging into one colour.

"What on Earth?"

Tarran stepped closer to see clearer.

"Careful Tarran," warned Morgan.

Ellie and Meadow entered with trays of food and a

bowlful of heather for George.

"Here you... Goodness, what is that?"

Meadow did a double take at the rocks as their colours swirled and moved into one another. Ellie gave a quick side glance at where Meadow was looking as she handed the plates of egg and chips round.

"My goodness!" she exclaimed.

They sat and watched the dancing colours of the stones merge into one another, eating and staring like a family watching television in the reality that now seemed far, far away. George scooped his hand down into the bowl, emerging with a handful of heather flowers before promptly putting the entire handful in his mouth, all the time staring at the hypnotic sight.

"You know what we need?" said Aunt Ellie, "I think we need a fire."

"Oh, Auntie Ellie, it's too warm. I know its Scotland but it is July, after all."

"No Tarran, not a human fire, but a dragon fire. This is Castle Seton."

Tarran's eyes widened.

"What? Dragon fire?"

Tarran's lack of knowledge was disconcerting. George once again realised how little they knew but was also rather peeved that he had not thought of this himself. Dragon fire was rare for a reason, and its uses were not always known. Hats off to the boy who had thought to use it. This wondrous sight before them needed a key to understand it, and none of them had guessed what it might be, except the boy. Well,

well, wonders never ceased.

"Aye, Ma. I think we definitely need a dragon fire," he replied sitting back in the huge chair, satisfied with his meal and even more satisfied at his clever little idea.

13. Dragon Fire

The Brownies were going to love the mess the witches and children were making. Even George contributed to the general untidiness whilst eating his heather flowers, allowing several leaves to fall on the floor.

"I did it deliberately," he whispered to Ava. "The brownies need something to clean."

Ava rolled her eyes at him in dismay.

Aunt Ellie brought out two small green and blue pieces of rock from a small wooden dragon shaped box.

"Of course, dragon flint," Meadow said, as if remembering some geology from school.

Aunt Ellie bent down towards the huge fireplace with its huge images of dragon heads and knights in armour carved into the green marble, otherwise known as dragon stone. She banged the two dragon flints together.

Two blue sparks from the flints appeared.

Moments later, a blue flame leapt from the flints and ignited the fire and the huge wooden log in the fireplace burned bright blue.

Ava held out her hand to it.

"There's no heat," she said to Tarran.

"None," he replied, holding his hands towards the flame.

"Now then Ellie, let's put these two in the dragon flame and see what happens. What do you think, George?"

"Can't hurt my lady," George replied, eager to see what would happen.

April moved towards Ava and put her arm round her protectively. Ellie lifted the stone of Seton from its special resting place and Winnie approached with the other. Each of them placed their stones in the blue flame and stepped back.

"So mote it be!"

They uttered these words and watched as aunts April and Meadow and George repeated, "So mote it be," after them.

Aunt Meadow stood next to her son as April's hand wrapped closer round Ava. George was by her side with Tarran and Morgan nearby.

Ellie and Winifred raised their hands upwards. As they did so, the flames grew higher. The rocks rose in the blue flames and were suspended above the fire, then swirled around each other, their silver and gold flecks merging into one until finally they collided in a loud explosion and the two rocks became a giant turquoise one. The gold and silver writing formed words and lines. Winifred turned to April and waved at her.

"Quick April, pen and paper."

April ran to Lord Seton's desk and grabbed his notebook and his writstar's pen. The gold and silver words took form gradually, shining brightly in the blue flames on the giant turquoise rock.

Aunt Winifred read them out as April meticulously wrote them down. Ava peered at the writing - it was rainbow coloured.

Winifred squinted her eyes as she read the emerging

words.

A sword of fire, a sword of flame…
Upon The Thirteen find a name…
A sword of kings, a sword of queens…
"I can't quite see…"
six of each the sword does keep…
"Oh the words are changing again, April."
and one … witch's soul… forever weeps!

The last line pierced through the witches like a knife slicing their hearts. Winifred winced as she read it and George placed his hand upon his heart and looked down towards the floor.

The fire crackled, hissed and spat, forcing Ellie and Winifred back, joining the rest as they watched the blue flame turn into an orange of great heat and intensity.

Meadow stood closer to her son, ready to protect him in an instant. George held on to Ava.

With a muffled explosion, the stone disintegrated in a flash as the flames disappeared leaving a pile of ashes in the fireplace.

"What happened? Where's the rock and the stone of Seton?"

"The magic is spent, Ava," George answered. "The stone has done its job. It is no longer needed."

"Right, April," said Winifred, commanding urgency, "what have we got? Read it out, sweetie."

April held the paper with trembling hands. She gulped.

A sword of fire, a sword of flame,
Upon The Thirteen find a name.
A sword of kings, a sword of queens,
Six of each the sword does keep,
And one witch's soul forever weeps.

"What does it mean Winnie?"

"I've absolutely no idea, but I intend to find out. Tarran and Meadow, you have the Latin wall please. Find anything you can on this. No clue, no matter how small is insignificant, every tiny piece of knowledge is worth investigataing.

"Morgan, Ellie, look up everything on the House Seton and their connections. George and Ava, search the less well known library books, and April you are with me, we must put our heads together and see what we can see."

It was neither an easy nor clear task, for any of them, but they scurried off to their designated areas.

Ava glanced round the library in consternation and said to George.

"Where do we start?"

George gave a gentle wave with both hands.

A mist appeared, as if a veil had descended upon them. Ava's skin felt the same as when she was last in Avalonia.

"George, are we still in the library?"

"Yes and no my lady. We are now riding the world's most secret books. They are known as corens and exist alongside their counterparts in the human world, but only those who are of Fae can see them and bring them into the human world."

"So, am I...?"

"You are both, Ava, Fae and human, from your Fae mother and your human father. Come now, let us search."

In front of the regular library books, like a misty, almost translucent veil, were rows and rows of floating books of Fae, drifting on unseen shelves, stacked as if in a library within a library.

In the centre of one such shelf was Berach, Light of Whisper, with what looked like a feather duster, cleaning the spines.

"Hello, Berach," said Ava. "You clean here, too?"

He turned and pulled his giant ear lobe three times.

"That means yes," George explained, leaning in close to Ava. "One pull means no, two means don't know and three means yes," he said whilst pulling on his own ear.

"Can they see us?" Ava asked, nodding towards Tarran and Meadow.

"Yes, but they can't hear or see what we can."

"How strange!"

"What is?" Morgan asked, looking up, his head deep in a book about the history and lineage of ancient dragons.

"Oh, nothing. Doesn't matter."

As she searched the suspended tomes, one caught her eye. It was called, *A Story of the Sea*, but as soon as she reached out to touch the book of air, it became real and solid. She could feel its and weight and heaviness.

"Wonderful, wonderful," she whispered, but not so softly that the others did not hear.

They looked up from their own searching to see what Ava had found so unusual.

"Where did you get that from?" Morgan asked.

"There are places in this library that even you do not know about, Morgan," said Winifred, and winked at Ava knowingly.

Ava reciprocated the knowing look to her aunt.

There was so much to learn and Ava felt a great sense of pride and power in the secret knowledge that was opening up to her in this most secret of places.

She looked at the book in her hands.

The picture on the front was a sea scene and it appeared to be moving. The waves rolled towards her and as she opened its pages, she could smell the sea and could feel the sea breeze on her skin. She started reading.

"Auntie, listen to this:

A Story of the Sea

Dragons flew upon the air riding unseen waves, whilst others dived into the watery depths as sirens called to them. Mermaids and dragons danced upon ocean currents as forests merged with the society of men.

Swords forged in this time were of earth, air, fire and water, but the greatest of all these was the immortal Sword of Rhyddech.

It was immortal because forged within it was the soul of a witch, the very first witch, tried and burned in Ireland. Her name was Petronilla de Meath. Her trial and subsequent punishment set a precedence for the rest of Europe and the emerging witch trials of the Medieval and Renaissance Periods.

However, unbeknown to historians, the real reason why Petronilla was killed concerned the Sword of the Immortals.

Six kings and six queens swords were thrown into the furnace of Draconia, and one witch's soul bound the sword together for eternity.

This is no ordinary sword.
This is a sword of the ages.
This is a sword of peace.
This is a sword that stops war.

No one said a word.

All was still within the grand library, yet in the distance was a sound, a deep earthy sound stemming from the castle itself.

Ava held her breath for a moment to listen to it but as she did so, she inadvertently slowed time.

The page that Tarran was turning stopped in mid-turn. As Morgan was about to close a book, his hands instead held the book in half. Winifred and Ellie stood motionless whilst the tea Meadow was pouring had slowed to almost complete stillness, just a slow trickle of tea found its way into the cup.

Time moved in drastically slow motion as the sound grew louder, a humming that resonated round the castle.

The louder and stronger it grew, the more the room seemed to vibrate, until it coalesced into shapes - small, stocky, brown shapes.

Brownies!

Brynmar appeared, with the others standing slightly behind him. Time corrected itself as Ava started breathing.

Morgan closed his book, for some reason looking incredibly sad. The sound was the brownies, all humming together. Brynmar sang in a low tone that made Morgan's skin tingle and the hairs on his neck stand to attention. It awakened something deep within him.

> *In sun and rain,*
> *We feel the pain.*
> *Of mountains mourn,*
> *Of human scorn,*
> *Till we are free,*
> *Till we can see*
> *All life that's born,*
> *Save earth's beauty.*

The song was accompanied by a communal humming and a soft singing of the melody. When they finished, their large heads lowered in sadness.

All was quiet in the library.

No one moved or seemed to breathe for that matter. Something quite profound had happened, and it took a while for the mood to lift. But it was not a profound word that brought them back to their senses.

The silence was broken when Aunt Ellie stood up, rather hurriedly, whispering to herself,

"Oh no, my honey cake!"

She dropped the books that had been on her knees and raced towards the kitchen, leaving the others to acknowledge the Brownie's song and its meaning.

14. The Immortals

The Brownies, still with their heads lowered as they finished their Earth hymn and lost in their own thoughts, did not see the Lord of the Castle approach. Morgan gently placed his hand on Brynmar's stocky shoulder. The Brownie gazed up at Morgan and blinked.

"You'll be needing this book then, Master Morgan."

An ancient book floated down from the highest part of the library turret. It was a long, thick book bound in blue and red leather. Its stitching had been white at some point but now it was faded to cream; time and wars had left their mark upon this fusty old tome.

Morgan opened his hands expectantly. The book hovered slightly above his palms before landing on them, softly and safely.

"*The Swords of the Union,*" Morgan read out, turning the pages.

No one said a word. Morgan glanced up from the book to the Brownies.

"Thank you, Brynmar. Thank you everyone. You make me happy."

Brynmar acknowledged this, as did the others. Not only did they blink at the same time, they did many things in unison, and now they faded away together, leaving only their delighted expressions behind before they too were gone.

Morgan, not distracted by the Brownies, read on.

The immortal sword of Rhyddech is the most powerful

sword of all ages. It was made in the fires of Draconia in the Age of Dragon. The swords of magic and the swords of humankind were forged together.

Six kings gave their swords to the King of Scotland, the Dragon Rider of Annandale.

The sword of King Alfred the Great
The sword of King Arthur
The sword of King Beowulf
The sword of King Richard, the Lionheart
The sword of King Gwnedd, Rhoddri the Great
The sword of King Robert the Bruce

In addition, with the kings' swords, the warrior Queens of the Union also gave their swords for the benefit of all:

The sword of the Queen Elizabeth I
The sword of Queen Aethelflaed, Lady of the Mercians
The sword of Queen Mary of Scotland
The sword of Queen Eleanor of Aquitane
The sword of Queen Nest of Wales
The sword of Queen Elen of Wales

These swords were thrown into the great fire of Draconia on a Midsummer's Eve, centuries ago, but the main component was the soul of the first witch of Ireland. It bound the swords together forever and is known as the immortal sword due to its power to invest immortality in whoever is struck by it on the Feast of Lammas on the night of a waxing moon. It can only be wielded by the Celtic Messiah.

Morgan slowly closed the book and waited for someone

to reply.

"I feel nervous and uncertain about all of this, auntie," said Ava, shaking her head. "I don't know why, I just do. It feels sad, like the beginning of the end."

Winifred placed her arms round her niece.

"Oh, my darling, never fear, we are all here for you. But make no mistake, this particular quest will bring us into direct contact with forces that are going to change us. I'm not ashamed in saying that I too fear what this battle will bring."

Tarran scratched his head. He was working something out again.

"Wait a minute. This can't be true about the sword. I mean all those kings and queens lived at different times. How can they all be present at once, if that is what the verse meant?"

"Because, Master Tarran, time is fluid. It can manifest everywhere and there are beings who can travel with time."

Commander George turned to Ava, who was still cuddling her Aunt Winifred who held onto her niece that bit harder.

"We've already seen that Queen Elizabeth was an ally of Fae. She helped hide the horn of Bran. Who's to say the others were not also allies to the elementals? Furthermore, those kings and queens you speak of, Master Morgan, are also known as the Immortals for they live on in another world and another time."

Tarran's thoughts ran round his busy head, thirteen to the dozen.

"Possibly, yes," then turning to the clue Aunt April had written down. "So, whose name is it? Upon The Thirteen find a name?"

"Petronilla de Meath," said April. "She is the thirteenth. *One witch's soul forever weeps*, remember? Petronilla is the key, she holds and binds the swords together."

"I'll go along with that, April, after all, it mentions six kings and six queens, although not by name, but *upon the thirteenth find a name*. Yes she is the thirteenth."

Meadow tapped the paper April was holding.

"We are going with Petronilla, yes? What do you think Ava? What do your instincts say, darling?"

Ava buried her head into her aunt's warm body before replying.

"There is a name that keeps popping into my head, but it's not Petronilla, it's Aethelflaed."

"Let's see what happens, shall we?" said Winifred. "Keep both the names in our heads and when the right moment arises, we'll speak of it. Right now, I think we need an early night. Don't know about you all, but I'm totally zonked. It's been a productive but exhausting day."

"I couldn't agree with you more, Winnie," said Ellie. "Let me show you to your rooms. Morgan, show Ava and Tarran where their rooms are please. Come on ladies, follow me."

Ellie escorted everyone out of the library, leaving it in a frightful mess. Books and plates were strewn everywhere, along with cushions and throws, used by all during the extensive research.

The Brownies were skipping with delight at the mess they were going to have to clear. Ellie said,

"Thank you, my friends, there is fresh honey cake for you all in the kitchen for keeping the house so wonderfully clean while we've been away."

The Brownies acknowledged this praise in their usual synchronised way and, grabbing a dirty plate each, disappeared into the kitchen for their reward.

15. The Castle and the Mermaid

The forests whether water or land grown,
Of earth and sea, of wood or oceans' foam,
Forests reign supreme,
Devoted eternally to our Queen.

"Here Ava, you can have the turret bedroom. It faces south and I think you get the best views from here," Morgan proudly explained while opening the door to a beautiful room with a four-poster bed and wooden carvings of ships, sea, mermaids and dragons.

The yellow and grey tartan carpet and curtains matched the yellow wall and brightened the oak carvings and bed.

"Wow, Morgan, not too shabby!" exclaimed Ava.

"Come on, this is your bathroom with some of Aunt Lexi's special bath bombs, of course."

"Special?"

"Aye, the red ones help you swim with dragons whilst the blue ones help you to swim with mermaids."

Tarran's eyes widened.

"Come on Morgan, where's my room? Have I got something 'special', too?"

Morgan could only manage Goodnight Ava, before being pulled away by Tarran.

Closing the door after them, she saw Morgan put Tarran in a headlock as they scrambled down the corridor to a bedroom on the other died of the hall. Ava shut the door, alone with her thoughts. George was around but had chosen to hang out with the Brownies downstairs.

"I wonder if he misses home?" Ava mused while running a bath.

She held the red bath bomb in one hand and the blue one in another. She hadn't seen Mariella for a while and without thinking, she tossed the blue bath ball into the water. No sooner had she done so than the water bubbled, fizzled and turned blue.

Ava couldn't wait to dive in. She tested the bubbling and fizzing water and thought she would touch the bottom of the bath with her hand… but it wasn't there! She leaned further and further in until her whole arm was up to her shoulder and her face almost touching the water.

A hand reached out and pulled her in.

Ava gulped a lung full of air and kept her eyes closed. She could feel herself being pulled through the water at an almighty rate. The water wasn't cold, nor hot, it was just right. Her hand was being held tight and something pushed past softly on her skin as she swam through the water until finally she slowed down.

"Ava open your eyes. You must open your eyes Ava or you will miss the beauty all around you."

Cautiously, she opened her eyes. The salt water stung them for a bit but as she blinked, they grew more focused and she beheld the wonder around her.

There was Mariella, the Princess of the Ocean, the mermaid of the sea. Ava had never seen her completely in water before, only in the Castle at Avalonia and then again on the Orkney Islands at Midsummer with Aunt Jissika. She had legs then, but now she appeared in all her beautiful, majestic mermaid wonder.

Her tail was turquoise with green, gold and indigo scales. It was a huge tail. Ava had no idea a mermaid's tale could be this long. Her hair flowed around her in the ocean currents.

"Welcome to my home."

Mariella waved her hand for Ava to view the sight before her. A magnificent world of ancient buildings and glowing lights with hundreds of mer people all swimming elegantly around.

"Follow me."

Ava swam as best she could after Mariella who glided through the water with the softest movements of her huge tail.

Tall sea grass and sargassum swayed outside the underwater city gates.

"Where are we, Mariella?"

"Somewhere off the North Atlantic."

"And how am I talking to you and breathing under water?"

"You are a child of fae, you were born in the Age of Selkie and you are a child of water. Come and meet my family."

As they swam under the coral gates of a magnificent city of blue, pinks and turquoise coral buildings with iridescent lights shining through them, the mer people stopped swimming and bowed their heads to ackowledge them.

"Here are my sisters."

Seven mermaid sisters greeted her. One brought her a necklace made from different coloured sea glass, interspersed with pearls.

"Thank you so much. It's beautiful."

"You are always welcome here, Ava. The mer people are your allies. Call upon us whenever you need."

"Thank you, thank you. But as much as I would love to stay, I think I need to be getting back now."

"Of course, follow me."

Mariella glided through the city as her sisters waved goodbye. Once outside, she said,

"Hold my hand tightly now."

"Why?"

"Because we are going to swim the current of life, or as you would call it, the Gulf Stream."

Ava reached out her hand to feel the cool fingers clasp around hers. Mariella gave one strong stroke of her tail and whoosh, they were away!

She tried to catch her breath as they sped through the current, looking up to see a light. Mariella loosened her grip and let go. Ava turned to see her waving.

"See you again, Ava."

She twisted round and round in the current. The light was getting closer until she broke the surface, gasped the air and found herself... back in the bath again.

She touched the sea glass and pearl necklace to make sure that what had happened had truly happened.

It was there.

She looked at it carefully. It was as wonderful here as it

had been in the deep sea, off the Atlantic coast. How mind boggling was that to consider!

She lay back and allowed her mind to recall the fleeting beauty of what she had seen. How could she tell anyone about it? They would never believe her – unless they saw the necklace, and even then… But it didn't matter. Mariella was real, her sisters were real and the friendship of the Mer people was real.

Laughing softly, Ava played with the bubbles and foam of the bathwater.

16. The Castle Secrets

The events of last night had sent Ava into a deep sleep, so much so that she awoke next morning with Morgan and Tarran shaking her.

"What the…"

"Come on Ava, I want to show you something."

Ava rubbed her eyes.

"Are the others up?"

She glanced at the curtains; it was barely light.

"What time is it?"

"It's just dawn. Come on Ava, get ready or we'll miss him."

"Miss who? Oh no, we are not travelling by dawn's light again, are we?"

"No fear, but we need to go now."

Clambering out of bed, Ava slipped her feet into her flip flops and ruffled her hair. Morgan was practically bouncing with excitement. He raced ahead of Ava and Tarran, down endless stone steps until they reached the very centre of the Earth, or so it felt.

What light there was dimmed to darkness in the bowels of the castle. The air grew colder and a smell of the sea permeated upwards.

Finally, Morgan jumped down the last couple of stairs to land on sandy gravel. Tarran held out his hand for Ava to hold onto as she approached this lowest level.

"Where are we?"

"It looks like we are under the castle in a cave with

direct access to the sea."

"Precisely, my good man," said Morgan.

Ava blinked her eye a couple of times to acclimatise. Tarran was right, it was a cave close to the sea, a twisting, turning cave with forbidding entrances and exits. The walls were draped with fresh seaweed and the ground was wet. The tide must have just gone out. The walls were formed of black shiny stone; Ava saw herself reflected in them.

"Black mirrors," she whispered.

"No, obsidian," answered Morgan.

The walls looked like they had been polished within an inch of their lives. 'Perhaps The Brownies had been here, too', thought Ava.

Turning a corner, at the far end of the cave, Samphire was playing ball with what looked like a seal. As she walked closer, she could see that this seal had arms and a ridiculously cute seal face with long brown hair, but a seal's body.

On seeing the trio approach, the seal jumped into the little pool of water and promptly popped her head up halfway. Only her large pretty eyes could be seen as she blinked looking at them.

"It's okay, Selkie, it's just me, Morgan with Tarran and Ava."

Selkie's head came out of the water a bit further.

Samphire, upon seeing Morgan, came bounding up to them, wagging his giant green tail and knocking dragon seats off the wall.

There were at least twenty different seats hung on the

rockface, like leather tapestries. They had different designs and different colours and shades from blue to red to green. Some of the straps were beautifully embossed with gold and silver inlays and rows of medieval patterns.

"Steady Samphire, steady."

"Look Morgan, they're dragon seats."

"Aye, I know that now, but didn't when I was here last. I just thought they were medieval kites."

"Are you going to try riding Samphire?"

Morgan scratched under Samphire's chin as he was clearly enjoying it. His eyes were closed tightly and every so often he would move his head so Morgan could scratch another area.

"I don't know, Ma said no."

Ava and Tarran both raised an eyebrow in disbelief.

"I know, I know. I have never listened to my mother so why bother now, eh?"

On the other side of cave, just up above Selkie's head was a long, oak shelf. Sitting on the shelf were rocks which looked similar to the Stone of Seton, but they were multi-coloured like rainbows flecked with gold.

"What are they, Morgan?" Ava asked in a low voice. She did not want to appear ignorant in front of the dragon.

"Dragon's eggs."

Tarran's eyes widened.

"You mean there are baby dragons inside?"

"Aye."

"How do they hatch?"

"They hatch from dragon fire. Dragons mature when

they are about five hundred years old. Samphire here is only two hundred and fifdty years old, aren't you boy, eh?" Morgan fussed over Samphire who was relishing all the attention. "Apparently, legend has it that only one dragon is alive in the world at any one time, and when that dragon reaches two hundred and fifty years of age, he can perform the *Anail na Beatha* ceremony, which is seen only during the Lammas festival."

"And?"

"And the dragon at Lammas breathes fire onto the dragon egg, that's what it means, Breath of Life, *Anail na Beatha.* But only the breath of dragon's fire can ignite the life inside the egg and only at Lammas which praises the last of the summer sun's power."

"Wow! Are we going to see it?"

"I don't know, it's all up to you isn't it, Sammy?"

"Sammy? He's not a spaniel Morgan, he is King Samphire."

"Aye, but he's also my Sammy, aren't you boy, eh? Yes, yes, you are!" Morgan played with Samphire even more.

Ava rolled her eyes and Tarran raised his eyebrow. Whatever Morgan thought, Samphire was still a wild creature. Ava wondered how much of this the creature would take. It was almost impossible to imagine him fierce and hostile, but he was who he was, and Ava would not want to get on his bad side. She doubted whether Samphire would be quelled by enemies tickling it under its scaly, scalding chin.

She walked over towards the eggs, passing Selkie in the

water who watched her intensely.

"Hello, Selkie."

Selkie made a little squeak like a curious, enquiring puppy. Ava reached out her hand. Selkie lifted her head out the water and sniffed.

"I wonder if you know Mariella?" Ava asked.

Whatever Ava was expecting, this wasn't it. As soon as Mariella's name was mentioned, Selkie's expression changed and she growled.

"Oh, don't you like her, Selkie?"

Selkie gave out a loud bark, shattering the pleasant scene, and dived down into the depths of the pool. Ava turned to the others.

"What on Earth was that all about?"

"The Mer-people and Selkie's people don't exactly get along."

"Indeed, they don't," replied a fourth voice.

Ava glanced around to see who was talking.

"They do not get along my Lady for the sole reason that during the Battle of Ages, the Mer-people betrayed Selkie's."

George materialised in front of them. He was dressed in his green tartan and tweed riding attire, complete with a pheasant's feather in his jacket pocket.

There was a whole hidden history here of species fighting species. Ava could see that now. How lucky Morgan was that Samphire's folk were loyal to the Fae, and especially to his family. If they hadn't been, he would not be free to tickle the dragon so freely. Who knew what other alliances and friendships existed that Ava knew nothing about. She had to learn, and to learn fast. Knowledge was power, especially so here.

"Going riding George?"

"No, my Lord Seton," George replied, "but you are."

17. Dragon Rider

George snapped his fingers and instantly Morgan was transformed into a medieval nobleman with thigh high black leather boots, white crisp linen shirt and a deep burgundy velvet long riding jacked embroidered with gold dragons on either side of its centre fastenings.

Ava giggled but Morgan approved.

"Now this I like George, well done."

George bowed in humble modesty. Even Tarran had to agree.

"Yep, definitely Morgan, you look the biz."

"Come, Master Morgan, we need to learn to ride Samphire."

"But Aunt Ellie had said no," objected Ava.

"I'm well aware of that Ava, however, I suspect we no longer have the freedom of ignorance. The enemy is all too aware of what we are capable of and therefore they will be waiting for us. Quite frankly, it's all hands on deck. If we start training now, Master Morgan, when the final battle comes you will be ready. Besides, with regarding one's parents or life in general, just do it. And in this case, we will have to ask for forgiveness rather than permission. Now then, let's saddle up. Bleddyn Sky of Thorne and Berach Light of Whisper, I call you forth to serve your Master."

No sooner had George uttered their names than the two Brownies appeared side by side. Upon seeing Morgan in his riding best, they both bowed extremely respectfully.

"Morgan, Bleddyn and Berach are your Grooms of the

Dragon. They have served your family since the beginning and know how to saddle Samphire. They will help and advise you. Listen wisely and let them guide you."

George then turned to the immaculately dressed Brownies.

"My Lords of the Dragon Grooms, if you would be so kind as to saddle his majesty King Samphire. Thank you."

"But George," said Ava, "Samphire is so big and - no offence, Bleddyn and Berach - they are really small. How on Earth are they going to fit a huge dragon seat on Samphire?"

"Just wait and see, my Lady."

A green dragon seat hanging on the rockwall floated across the cave towards Samphire. Its long flank cinch wrapped around Samphire who kept turning his head on either side of the girth and latigo.

Bleddyn stood on one side fixing the saddle while Berach stood on the other side of Samphire who appeared to be as equally intrigued as the humans at the show going on, of which he was the star attraction.

They fixed the cantle and adjusted the skirt and rear housing to accommodate Samphire's protruding spine scales on his back and he gave a little wiggle.

George scoffed, "Mmm, ticklish!"

Morgan gave him a sharp glance.

"Its not hurting him is it?"

"No, of course not. It's made of the softest leather known. Indeed, dragon saddles are made with the dragon in mind, not the rider. It will be alright for Samphire, not too sure about you, though."

As the last buckle was tightened, both Bleddyn and Berach stood back. Samphire gave a shake and admired himself in the obsidian walls of the castle cave.

"Right, do we need to go outside?"

"No, Master Morgan right here will do just fine for now."

"But he needs to fly?"

"First, you need to climb on board, as it were. Bleddyn, could you bring the stairway please? Come along, Samphire, this way."

Samphire stopped admiring himself and turned around so he was facing the opening of the cave. Manoeuvring a dragon in a cave was quite an accomplishment, to say the least! Samphire stood staring out to sea as Bleddyn materialised a crooked staircase, shaped like a giant 'L'. It was made from wood and had nooks and knots all the way through it like a knobbly finger. It reached across the deep pool to Samphire on the other side.

"Why not have a step up to Samphire on the opposite side?" Ava asked, fascinated.

"Because, my Lady Ava, one always mounts a dragon on the left."

"Why?"

"You'll see! Now Master Morgan, kindly start your climb to mount Samphire."

Morgan grabbed both sides of the rails. Halfway across, Samphire started wriggling and the staircase shifted slightly. Morgan's expression was one of concern as he held on tight to the wooden railings. He was directly above the water with about a twenty-foot drop straight down.

"Carry on, Master Morgan. He is a dragon after all and he will move."

Morgan continued cautiously across the staircase. He reached out to touch Samphire and felt his hard scales, like warm hard stone, but he could also feel the life force and power flowing through him.

Morgan lifted his leg over to the other side when Samphire sneezed, lurched forward, knocking Morgan off, straight into the pool. He hit the water with an almighty splash.

"And that my Lady, is why we learn to ride over the sea and why we mount dragons over water."

Tarran, in fits of hysterics went to help Morgan out of the pool. As he yanked Morgan up he stopped laughing. He touched Morgan's jacket.

"You're not wet!"

"What? Of course I am, I've just been in the sea. I am soaking."

He patted himself down, expecting to hear soft squelching sounds. Instead, his clothes, boots and pants were completely dry.

"What the…"

"A dragon rider's clothes are rather special, Master Morgan. No matter how many times you end up in the water, they will remain dry. These clothes are made in Fae, and as you know, everything made in Fae has a certain je ne sais quoi. Now then, Master Morgan, up the wooden stairs we go again."

Bleddyn and Berach stood close by, knowing their duties well. Bleddyn stood by the staircase and Berach stood by Samphire, gently patting him.

It was only his second attempt but already Morgan was more wary. He just wanted to reach the seat, hold tight and take to the skies.

"When do I start flying?" he asked, impatiently.

George answered immediately.

"When you can sit on him without falling off!"

18. The High Priestess

Watching Morgan ascending and descending the stairs grew tedious, at least for Ava. Tarran, on the other hand, found it equally funny each time Morgan plummeted into the cold sea. Ava decided to leave the scene and ventured back up the stone staircase.

"Where are you going, my Lady?" George asked.

"I thought I'd see what auntie is up to."

"You don't need to go that way, unless you like the dark, the damp and the exercise. You can walk along the beach and up the secret steps to the castle. Well, I say secret, but everyone knows about them." George pointed towards the mouth of the cave adding, "I shall go with you. Master Morgan, listen well to your Lords of the Dragon Grooms. Don't give up, and try to stay on, just once."

"Good luck, Morgan," said Ava. "Can't wait to see you fly."

"Aye, neither can I."

Samphire bowed his head to George who returned the gesture as he left the cave.

As they walked across the rugged beach of rockpools, overshadowed by huge cliffs and the looming presence of the dominating castle, Ava stared out to sea and asked George, "I wonder where Selkie lives?"

"Could be anywhere and everywhere, Ava. Mer-folk have their homes and cities in the oceans but Selkies tend to stay in one place, near their friends, perhaps."

"Doesn't she have any family?"

"No, my Lady, they were all killed when they were betrayed by Mariella's sisters."

George could see the concern on Ava's face.

"Far be it from me to gossip about another member of Fae but remember what the King said, Ava - trust no-one."

Ava stopped walking.

"Including you George?"

"Of course not, my Lady! I would sooner venture into the Summerlands than hurt you."

"I thought so George. I shouldn't have asked. I can't really obey the king in that respect, can I? No one could. I will always trust you - and Morgan and Tarran and my aunts. I trust more people than I don't, I think."

The seagulls squawked and soared up above them and every so often, as Ava looked out to sea, she thought she caught a glimpse of Selkie's head bobbing up and down intermittently, following them.

Rounding a giant black rock, Ava heard voices carried on the breeze, but she couldn't see where they were coming from.

"That sounds like Aunts Ellie and April," she whispered to George as she pulled him behind the rock with her.

"What are we doing behind here?"

"Shh!"

"Are we spying on our kinswomen?"

"No, not spying," Ava whispered. "Eavesdropping."

George raised one eyebrow in disgust.

"We fairies never eavesdrop!" Ava shot him a sharp glance but he added, "We spy!"

Ava shook her head and put her index finger up to her tightly closed lips. "Shh!" she said as she strained her ears to listen.

Aunts Ellie and April were making their way down the Secret Steps.

"I'm telling Ellie," April was saying, "she never changes unless there are Dark Fae energies nearby, and I'm convinced there are."

"Nonsense, mon cher April, the castle is protected. We have a Commander of Fae, a High Priestess, three witches, six Brownies and a dragon for crying out loud. There is no way that the Dark Fae could make their way inside or even pass the moat. Remember, too, April, that there is a doorway to her world, an escape."

"Yes, yes, and that's the other thing. How on Earth are we meant to keep this from Ava? We are getting so close to her mother that I'm surprised she hasn't made an appearance by now."

The voices became clearer as they approached Ava and George. Ava peered round the rock so as not to be seen, but jumped back. The aunts were close.

"I'm telling you Ellie," April continued, "this will all end in tears, and Meadow seems oblivious to it all. I don't know what her problem is."

"Meadow is a great practical help in times of battle. Her medical knowledge surpasses even that of Winnie's. Now where did she go running off to?"

A large and unexpected growl came from behind them. Even George was startled. Ava turned, stepped back and

The High Priestess

leant upon the rock for support. George turned, too - and relaxed.

There in front of them was the biggest snow white wolf ever seen, with the brightest blue eyes tinged with flecks of yellow.

"My Lady Winifred, how fetching you look today."

The wolf continued to growl as Ava cowered closer to the rock and to George.

"Now, now my lady, Ava was not spying, she was just… 'eavesdropping'. I, on the other hand, was spying."

The wolf spoke.

"Thank you, George," it replied in half human half growl-speak.

Then it gave a loud bark and ran right past Ellie and April, up the Secret Steps.

"There she is!" said April. "Winifred, wait! Winnie! Come on Ellie."

"Oh, my old bones, I can't take much more of this! I'll meet you up the top April," Ellie replied as she levitated gently up to the top of the cliff.

"Was that Aunt Winifred?" Ava asked.

"Yes, I'm afraid it was. She must have sensed the presence of the Dark Fae."

Ava peered round the rock to see Aunt April chasing Winifred up the steps. Near the portcullis, at the entrance of the castle, an unimpressed Aunt Ellie stood waiting with her arms crossed.

"Are we in danger here?" Ava asked.

"I doubt it," George replied, "but nevertheless, let's

make our way back to the castle and see what's going on. Come along, up the Secret Steps we go."

Ava wondered why The Secret Steps were so called. She could see the first one quite clearly and she pointed this out to George. He didn't answer. Ava soon realised that after each step, the one beneath and the one above vanished. Gone. Totally invisible. It was only the fact that she knew the stairway was there that she could continue climbing, but she couldn't see what she was stepping on. Looking at the steps from a distance, they seemed to merge into the rock, camouflaged by nature itself.

"Ooh, George, perhaps they are seret, after all. I don't like this. They make me dizzy."

"Look straight ahead my Lady, and whatever you do, don't turn around. Keep your eyes firmly focused on me."

Ava remembered saying the exact same words to her father only a couple of days before, but he hadn't listened. Ava was determined not to make the same mistake and pressed her lips together, religiously following every step George took until they were finally and safely at the top.

19. Sailing

Winifred had changed back into her human form when Ava and caught up.

"Nice day for flying, auntie."

Ellie looked surprised but sensed something was amiss and remained quiet. Winnie did not look at all happy. She wore an expression of severity, te like of which Ava had never seen before.

"Ava," said Aunt Winifred, "I can tolerate most things, but I will not have my niece spying on family. Do you understand? There are no secrets between us."

Aunt Meadow coughed as she walked in on the scene while Aunt April almost choked on her Dundee cake. Winifred cut them both a stare. Her wolf eyes had not quite disappeared and she appeared even more formidable than usual when riled.

"Oh, really auntie?" said Ava, not giving way. "No secrets? Well, why did you change? Are we in danger? If I hadn't seen it with my own eyes, would you have told me that you transformed?"

"It is not your concern, Ava. Whatever I do, whatever any of us do, there must be trust between us, always. There can be no reason, none at all, for spying on each other. Does that answer your question?"

Ava folded her arms and sat down.

Winifred shook her head.

"I'm sorry, but I can't have you skulking off, doing what you did. We have enough enemies Ava to fight out there without fighting amongst ourselve. Do you understand?"

Ava did not speak.

"Now where are the others? Where are the boys?"

"Humph! Up to no good, I suspect."

Ava was bursting to tell them about Morgan trying to learn to ride Samphire, but given the speech Aunt Winifred had just made, she thought a little white lie of silence was best.

"George, could you locate them please? We need to be on our way to Castle Island at Loch Leven after the events of this morning."

"What events?"

"I can usually control my transformtion, but not when there is so much unrest and evil in the air. I could feel the Dark Fae close and I think we will meet more than just Jissika and Chay at Loch Leven. George, please find the boys quickly. We need to leave on the next tide."

"At once, my Lady."

Ava felt a pang of guilt, but when Tarran and Morgan appeared with their Grooms of the Dragon, the secret was out and there was nothing she could do.

"What did I tell you about dragon riding, boy? You are not ready."

"Well, the way he kept falling off Samphire, you are absolutely right, Aunt Ellie," Tarran mumbled as he caught his mother shaking her head at him while giving him a cheeky wink.

"No time to argue and chastise now, Ellie. To quote a famous human detective, the game is afoot and we need to get to work. I think Jissika and Chay may be in danger. We can't wait until tomorrow, we go now. We shall sail before Lammas festivals are upon us. Grab your things everyone, we're off."

Ava joined Tarran and Morgan upstairs, collecting their bags.

"Did you manage to stay on Samphire long enough to fly yet Morgan?"

"Not quite, but I did manage to get my leg over the other side of the saddle. I didn't quite make it sitting down, but I'll keep practising. I think Sammy's getting used to the idea now."

"I must say," said Tarran, "when you did manage to stay on him for more that a second, you looked quite imposing. I definitely wouldn't want to come up against you in battle."

"Thank you, my fawning earth-vexing flap-dragon."

"Ooh! That's a good one, you craven dizzy-eyed ratabane."

"For heaven's sake," scolded Ava, "See you both downstairs in five."

Ava grabbed her backpack and rammed the neatly folded clothes into it, along with her father's journal. She had begun writing up the journal regularly and it was important for her to keep it safe and up to date.

"Here we go again."

She took one last look round the bedroom and closed the door behind her.

The others were already waiting. Winifred still looked mightily miffed.

"We need to head down into the Castle's Dragon's Keep," said Winifred, "but something tells me you already know where that is. Never mind," Winifred continued, sensing their discomfort, "let's go."

Once more, they made their way down the long stone staircase to where they had all been just a few hours before. The air had changed. It felt colder, sharper. Ava could hear the waves lapping up the obsidian walls.

"The tide is in," said Winifred.

Ava saw the water lapping at the bottom step. Samphire was nowhere to be seen.

"I shall get the boat, my Lady," said George, and transformed into his fairy self.

Winifred addressed the others, waiting behind one another on the steps. She was still irritated.

"Wait here. George will put the gangway up so we can get on board without soaking ourselves."

A loud splash ws heard and then, "Welcome aboard ladies and gentlemen. The Merry Queen welcomes you all."

George had turned human again, this time dressed in a navy sailing uniform complete with gold brocade on the shoulders and chest. His white pants shone bright against the black boots. He looked like a sea captain from the eighteenth century.

"Thank you, Nelson," Morgan sniggered as he came aboard.

George squinted and clicked his fingers at them all, instantly changing Morgan from his dragon riding uniform to a deckhand with red and white crew neck shirt and loose blue trousers. Tarran appeared as a petty officer with a small navy jacket and straw hat. Ava did not escape either. She wore a blue and white striped jumper with white capri pants and a blue and white headscarf which swept her hair up to one side.

None of them seemed particularly happy.

"How come I'm the deck hand and he's the petty officer?"

George bowed to them.

"You're welcome," he said. "Cast off, Master Morgan, if you please."

He clicked his fingers a second time and the gangway disappeared.

The boat, to all intents and purposes, looked like a Tudor ship but it just had one deck and one triangular sail. The bow and stern were raised with the bow slightly higher.

"Will the tide take us out, auntie?"

"Out of the cave, at least. After that, we shall see."

"It will be good to sail around the coast. We might even see Selkie or Mariella."

"We're not going out to sea Ava. This is no normal tide. We shall be on a sea within a sea. Remember, this is a boat of Fae."

Morgan was busy taking commands from George. The boat floated out of the cave and as it did so, the water receded, leaving the cave walls dripping with seaweed and salty water once more.

On the side stood the Brownies all in a row sharing an expression of sadness. They blinked their big eyes in unison as Ellie shouted across, "Thank you, my friends, we shall see you all soon. Morgan and I won't stay away from the castle too long. We shall return as soon as we can."

"And we've left the place in an awful mess just for you!" Meadow added.

From a distance, it appeared as if they shared one huge smile, then they faded from sight.

Ava squinted as she left the darkness of the cave. The sun beamed down in a cloudless sky. She looked out to sea and noticed a deeper blue in amongst the waves.

"There, do you see it Meadow?" said April excitedly, pointing to what looked like a river within the sea.

"Yes, that's it. George, hard to starboard please. The channel is there."

George steered the boat towards the dark blue current of water as Morgan hoisted the sail.

"Let her right out, Master Morgan."

"Aye, aye captain."

No sooner had Morgan let the sail out than the boat drifted towards the indigo channel. The moment it touched the dark blue water, it lurched forward and whoosh, it throttled up and shot forward. The wind and spray danced on Ava's face like tiny stinging nettles as she turned to her aunts sitting calmly at the stern.

Aunt Winifred's hair flew wildly around as she closed her eyes to relish the experience which was truly wondrous.

The boat followed the conjured current, never venturing into the wilder sea beyond. It was blue within blue, water within water and calm within deadly danger. Ava once again realised how much power her aunts possessed and how little she herself knew. No wonder Winifred had been angry with her. She determined to be wiser in the future.

Meanwhile, she took in the wonder of the journey, as did Tarran who watched as Castle Seton grew rapidly smaller and smaller until it was completely out of sight.

20. Loch Leven

The air changed from a salty sting to a soft dew upon the skin. The sea receded further and further away as the river twisted and stretched inland. Mountains became prominent as seagulls gave way to eagles. The boat slowed down as George commanded Morgan to bring in the sail. As he did and although there was hardly any breeze, the boat still drifted onward.

The sounds of the sea and waves lapping against the boat seemed to disappear with the wind as the stillness and silence swooped down around them until there in front of them loomed a huge loch, in the centre of which was an island.

"Castle Island at Loch Leven," uttered Ellie under her breath, as if it were a shame to speak loud and shatter the quiet calm.

It was so still. Hers was the only voice, carried on the air, laying heavy upon it like the lingering evidence of humanity.

"It once housed Mary Queen of Scots who was imprisoned here."

"Mary Queen of Scots? But she is one of the Queens of the Sword?"

"Aye, it could well be here."

"Turn astern George, we need to dock over there near the Castle."

As they approached, Meadow grew anxiou and asked,

"Where are Jissika and Chay? They said they would

meet us here."

"We are early," said Winifred, "a day early."

The lake was completely still like a mirror of the sky in which clouds chased the sun amidst a blue watery heaven. She felt uneasy. This was 'living water' and something drew her to it like a magnet, but she feared what lay beneath.

The boat slowed as it came alongside the jetty. Morgan jumped across, landing firmly on the wooden gangway and promptly tied the boat up. He reached out his hand to his mother.

"Thank you, son. This is so unearthly quiet. Not liking this, April," she said.

"I know what you mean Ellie. We all do."

Ava was too focused on the loch to think about the Castle, which to her looked ruined and harmless. It still had its tower and keep but appeared derelict and deserted.

"Come along, this way," Winnie ordered them.

They cautiously followed George who appeared equally wary of the all-encompassing stillness. As they approached the Castle entrance, Morgan, in a hurry and walking quite fast, came to an abrupt stop as if he had bumped into something. "Ow!" He rubbed his head. "I wish I knew. I hit something, but there's nothing here."

Tarran put his hands into the thin, empty air and felt a solid structure.

"There is something here, Morgan. An invisible wall."

Winifred breathed a sigh of relief.

"Thank heavens, Jissika has set up an Unseen Barrier

Spell. It will do us no harm."

Leaning over the Keep's battlements, a face appeared and someone shouted down to them.

"Welcome! And not a moment too soon! We've been fighting them off since we arrived."

"Chay! Who have you been fighting?"

"Them," Chay pointed.

There wasn't anything obvious to be seen, but then the water in the loch rippled and bubbled.

"Hurry, hurry, come in. I'll raise the gate."

"What gate?" said Morgan. "There's nothing here. I just hit an invisible wall."

"Believe me there's a gate. Now continue coming towards us. Quickly!"

The water simmered and boiled. Hundreds of heads emerged - the Army of Lost Souls.

Ava had never seen them this close, but she could see them now, or at least what they once had been.

They were souls neither dead nor alive, the shells of people emptied of dreams. They held spears, axes and knives and they moved fast.

Their minds may have gone, yet they knew that there was nowhere to go but the castle, which was surrounded. Hundreds and thousands of lost souls emerged from the loch and surrounding hills, threatening Ava and the others.

"Ava, hurry yourself!"

Tarran grabbed her and ran through the conjured gate. One of the souls emerging from the depths stared right into her – it was as if a cold knife had slid into her heart.

"Robin Goodfellow!" she whispered in horror.

She roused herself and sprinted into the castle.

The gate closed and the atmosphere shifted. A threat still hung in the air, but Ava felt protected. It was as if she had flown back in time to a medieval siege. Fires were lit and thousands of dragonflies were standing guard.

"General Ignatius," said George, and the two bowed to one another.

Jissika came to greet them.

"Thank the gods you are here. They've been attacking us since we arrived. We can't hold them off much longer."

"What do they want?"

"The same things as you do, I suspect."

"The Sword of Rhyddech! Is it here?"

"Sadly no," said Chay, welcoming Morgan and Tarran. "We've searched for it, but nothing."

Chay had grown since the last time Ava had seem him. He was as tall and willowy as Tarran though not as stocky as Morgan. His mousy hair was longer and he kept it off his face with two braids on either side, fastened by turquoise beads. His clothes were loose and his tunic bore geometric designs. He wore leather bracelets on his wrist with engravings of Inuit warriors.

"What are they doing here?" Winifred asked, puzzled. "There's more to this Jissika, I can feel it."

"I know what you mean, Winnie. I think they've been waiting for you. I think they're after Ava."

"Well, they're not going to get her," George answered, coming closer to Ava, letting her know how well she was protected.

"I'm afraid we need to fight them if we are going to get out of here alive, Winnie," said Jissika.

The light faded, unaturally fast, unnaurally dark. A heaviness weighed them down. Chay and Jissika both shouted in unison, "Battle stations! Posts everyone!"

General Ignatius flew to his command as did George, Meadow and Ellie.

"You know who we need for this, April," said Jissika. "Welsh wizardry."

"Right Jess, I'll call him. Which one is the Western Fire?"

"That one," she shouted as she ran to join the readying fray.

Chay headed in the opposite direction ushering Morgan and Tarran to support different corners of the castle.

"Come along Ava, let's keep you safe."

"I don't want to be safe. I can fight."

"I know, and you will, but you don't need to be in the front line," Winifred answered, almost dragging her up to the Tower battlements.

George and Winifred stood on either side of Ava as Aunt April whispered something into a glowing torch. She could not hear what April was saying but she could see the flames rise higher and higher into the sky and spread along the emerging clouds.

The loud buzzing of thousands of dragonfly wings could be heard as they flew to position in neat rows on every side of the castle.

In the distance, over the mountains in the darkening sky, Ava watched an ominously large mass drifting in towards them. It was far away, but the threat was evident.

"What is it, George?"

George studied the shadowy shape, shimmering and shifting on the horizon.

"It is the enemy, my Lady. It is the thing we are here to fight. It is the Nothingness."

21. The Lady Rises

The darkness swooped down over the land and loch like a devouring plague leaving nothing in its wake except emptiness. The Army of the Lost Souls moved towards the castle. Any of their number that fell in the attack only succeeded in creating steps for others to reach their goal. And what was their goal but to find and take Ava. As more fell from arrows, spears and spells, so more souls rose from the earth, surrounding the island.

A flash of bright purple. The loch bubbled and rippled.

"No more!" Ava cried out, but there was more.

Day became night and coldness filled the air. The Dark Fae emerged with penetrating blood red eyes searching for prey to curse and torment.

Ava sought out Aunt Winifred but she had disappeared.

"Where is she, George?"

"Where do you think, my Lady?"

The noise of the battle was deafening. The voices of the living, the cries of the dying, the clash of metal on metal, the swoosh of arrows, the beat of dragonfly wings and the confusing shouts of command. In amongst the chaos was an almighty shriek, heard across the sky, radiating throughout the air.

A flash of red amongst the black of the Nothingness. A plume of fire streaking across the mountains, flames shooting into the sky. The Nothingness ceased moving.

April ran up to the battlements.

"Isn't he magnificent, Ava? It's King Eryri, the last air

dragon of Wales."

As he swooped past them on his fly-by, April and George bowed to him.

"Now that's a dragon!" exclaimed Tarran.

Indeed, he was everything a dragon from legend could be. His piercing orange eyes matched the fierceness of the flames shooting from his mouth as his fire lit up the darkened day.

Fire and light stopped the Nothingness but it did not hold the Army of Lost Souls led by Robin Goodfellow.

The battlements were breached by the Dark Fae and the lost souls as thousands of corpses created an unholy staircase to their ultimate prize.

A repulsive Dark Fae ran at Ava when a flash of white fur jumped over her, grabbed the creature by its throat and shook it ferociously.

Winifred had become the wolf.

As it threw the remains of the Dark Fae over the battlements, the wolf gazed at Ava who could not hold its fercious stare. The wolf turned away to maintain its onslaught on the enemy.

"Come, my Lady, this way," George called, grabbing Ava, but it was too late.

Behind, a host of lost souls separated him from Ava.

Morgan leaped over to her from his side of the battlments just as Ava found herself face to face with Robin Goodfellow.

"Ah, Lady, we meet again. Now you will come with us or die here right now."

"I'd sooner die," Ava replied.

"Your wish is my command," said the foul creature. "Nothing would give me greater pleasure," and brandishing a glinting dagger raised it high to thrust it down.

Morgan cried aloud, "Nooo!"

The dagger pierced Morgan who crumbled to the floor.

Goodfellow grabbed Ava.

"No matter, you are coming with me, my Lady."

Ava could not take in what had happened. Her face drained of all colour. Was it all to end like this, in shame and defeat?

From the loch, a figure emerged grasping a sword of flame. She was dressed in white with long flowing silver hair that reached down into the water and she moved across the loch with astonishing speed. She was neither fae nor human. She was an Ancient and she did not fear Robin Goodfellow. She towered over him, awful and unstoppable.

"Let go of my daughter!" she bellowed, thrusting the flaming Sword of Rhyddech right through Robin Goodfellow.

"Melusine!" was all Goodfellow could say as he fell and faded.

The army and the Dark Fae, seeing both their leader and the Nothingness beaten, retreated.

Ava, shaken but unharmed, cradled Morgan's head in her lap. The Lady handed the flaming sword to George and knelt down beside Morgan, pulling the dagger from his wound. He screamed in pain, but at least he was alive.

Ellie and Meadow came running, then froze as they

witnessed the Lady of the Lake tend to Morgan. She poured water from her hands over his wound and the healing waters washed the blood away. The wound grew smaller and smaller until the blood and pain were washed completely away.

Morgan opened his eyes and gazed upon The Lady, hovering over him. He did not seem to know where he was or what had happened. At the same moment, Winifred joined them, holding her hand to her side. In a weak voice, all she could say was, "Ava."

Morgan recovered his senses slowly as Ava helped him to sit up. The Lady of the Lake reached out her hand to Ava who felt love and all it meant revive her. She stared at the lady but could not speak. Her mother! She studied every part of her face. It was timeless, with porcelain skin and the deepest blue eyes. Her white blonde hair was twice as long as she was tall and flowed free in the breeze. She was stunning and all Ava could say was, "Mother."

Tarran and April joined them, longing to know if they were all well. They saw The Lady of the Lake take the sword from George and place it in Ava's hands.

"Here, my darling, I believe this is what you seek. Guard it well and when this is all over, come find me."

She bent down, giving Ava a kiss on her forehead, then turned to Winifred who bowed to her.

"Thank you, High Priestess, for taking care of my daughter. Blessings upon you this Lammas."

"Thank you, my Lady Melusine, blessings to you too."

Addressing them all, she added, "I grant you safe

passage by river and water. Know always, Ava, you are my beloved daughter and I shall never fail you, nor you me. Time and tide are our nature, you and I."

The Lady then glided gracefully back to the loch where she descended into the watery depths. The clouds and darkness lifted as blue skies returned and a ray of sun shone down upon the water. A flap of huge wings wafted waves of air around them as King Eryri landed on the tower.

"Diolch frenin Eryri."

April bowed to the dragon king who surveyed the area and, seeing that there was nothing more he could do, took flight once more back home to Wales.

Ellie hugged Morgan giving him a massive cuddle and would not let go of him.

"Ma," squirmed Morgan trying to break free from his mother's clutches. "I am healed. Truly. Let me breathe!"

"Are you alright, Ava?" asked Tarran.

She didn't know what or how to answer.

"We were fortunate," said George, "and brave, of course, but it is back to Candlesby, methinks. Lammas beckons. Will you be joining us this year, my Lady Jissika?"

"Oh yes, George. I wouldn't miss this for the world."

"All aboard, then."

"Thank you, General Ignatius," said Chay. "I will see you back at Candlesby."

The little dragonfly gave a salute and flew upwards followed by his tens of thousands of troops. George led the way back down to the waiting boat leaving Ava and her aunt standing alone on the battlements. Aunt Winifred broke the silence.

"Brave girl. And you have the sword."

"Yes," Ava tightened her grip. "Did you know my mother had it?"

"Not for certain. I knew there was a connection but that was all."

"Is she truly the Lady of the Lake?"

"Amongst other names, and she can appear in many forms, wherever there is water."

"Who is she, auntie? What is she?"

"Remember what I told you at Midsummer, she is Melusine, an ancient water goddess, that is why time and tide are a part of you."

"Will I see her again?"

Winifred placed her hand on Ava's shoulder.

"I'm sure she will make her presence known again to you now, when she is ready. She will never be that far away. She must have been watching over you all this time and when you were in real danger, she came to save you. She's rather formidable, isn't she?"

Ava gave a nervous laugh.

"She's terrifying."

"Yes, and that's her on a good day!"

"So are you, auntie."

"Am I? It's always hard to see oneself as others see you. But like your mother, I am always on your side... most of the time, at least. Come on sweetie, let's get that sword back to Candlesby for safe keeping."

Ava carried the sword in her arms like a baby, walking towards the boat. Holding the sword, she felt a strong and vital connection to her mother, the same force flowing through its mysterious metal as it flowed through them both.

22. Lammas Fair

The Merry Queen graced the rivers of Scotland on her journey south. Morgan showed Chay how to hoist the sails.

"I'm more of a land person Morgan, but something tells me you will soon be airborne," said Chay.

Tarran sat next to Ava admiring the sword still cradled in her arms.

"Do you think this could be the sword of legend, Excalibur?" he asked Chay.

"Quite possibly, Master Tarran, all myths have an element of truth in them."

The sword reflected the sun's rays as they danced off the shimmering water. It was gorgeous, the most exquisite design, filled with mystery and history.

As they crossed the border into England, the air became warmer. Ava imagined the river's tide flowing through time as well as space. The gentle sway of the boat rocked her softly and somewhere in between waking and sleeping, she closed her eyes.

A mist ascended from the water's edge. Along the riverbank, the Queens of the Sword stood to watch them pass, but only Ava could see them as they drifted downstream to Candlesby. The last of the line was Aethelflaed who held aloft another sword, pointed it at an empty part of the riverbank and immediately a hedgerow of briar roses appeared, lining the way to Candlesby Manor. It was another wondrous sight. Ava waved, slightly nervously, sensing that she would see the queen again, that she would see them all again.

They neared Candlesby Manor and the Merry Queen seemed somehow to shrink, accommodating the brook at Candlesby leading directly to the heart of the forest.

Although weary from battle, they rejoiced at being back home. The Heart of the Forest had been decorated in the colours of Lammas. In the grounds, a great fair had been set up with stalls and entertainment. Distant music played and carried on the breeze as they stepped onto Candlesby land.

"Home sweet home," said Aunt Winifred. "The place looks marvellous," she added.

All around them were beings of Fae, from fauns to fairies to six lovely little Brownies all dressed in their finest clothes.

"Bleddyn, Berach, Florry, Brynmar, Bedwyn and Swann Merry!" Morgan greeted them. "My dear friends, so good of you to come, but why are you here?"

They all looked up over Morgan's head as a familiar shadow loomed over him. He turned to see the big green eyes of Samphire. Bedwyn stepped forward holding a highly polished dragon's egg in his hands. Morgan knew immediately what it meant. "Really?"

"Yes, absolutely," came the reply as Wolfe, Marsden and Bram came bounding up to them, laughing and joking and patting each other on the back.

Chay came forward and Wolfe put his hands together in prayer anmd in jest, as if to greet him.

"Welcome, Chay."

Chay responded with an embrace.

"How are you all?" he asked. "Pleased to see me?"

They laughed when Bram said of Chay's clothes, "Oh, love the beads Chay."

"Thank you, Bram, I will make you some if you like."

"We thought you wouldn't make it Winnie," said Guinevere, "it is Lammas, after all."

"Is it? Surely we have two days left before Lammas."

"No, it's Lammas right now, and the setting sun today is the last of Summer's power. It will soon be too late for the Anail na Beatha ceremony."

"How did that happen?" Ava asked.

"Time and tide, my Lady Ava, time and tide," said George.

"Come now, come quickly Fae, fauns, elementals and humans alike to the Heart of the Forest."

The last of the sun's rays were just disappearing over the trees as Samphire breathed a blue flame of fire onto the dragon's egg. He seemed to breathe on it for ages until it glowed with a blue heat of its own.

The witches and fae danced around it as the moon came out. Ava walked towards the manor leaving the merry making behind.

"My Lady," said George, "where are you going? It's the Lammas festival, come and enjoy."

"I'm tired George, and I need to put the sword away safely."

"I will accompany you."

"It's no bother really."

"Indeed, but I enjoy your company, my Lady."

"Of course," said Ava, "nothing would give me greater pleasure."

They walked silently back to the manor leaving the festivities. George opened the door to the secret room and watched Ava place the sword next to the horn of Bram. She smoothed her hands over it and thought back to Midsummer and how many changes she had gone through. It seemed so long ago.

"I'm tired George. I will say goodnight."

"Then I will take my leave, my Lady, and return to the merry making."

"Goodnight George, and thank you."

She watched him leave then opened the door to her bedroom. A welcome sight greeted her, for there on her bed was a wagging tail and big brown eyes.

"Jennifer!" she exclaimed, and lay down beside her. As soon as Ava's head hit the pillow, she drifted into a deep sleep, listening to the gentle lullaby of fairy music which played well into the night.

A green glow illuminated the darkness of her room and something peered through the window. The sound of beating wings woke her. When she flung open the curtains, two luminous green eyes peered at her.

"Samphire!" Ava exclaimed, before throwing the window open and reaching out to tickle his nose.

The dragon wagged his tail before bowing his head. As he did so, Ava could see none other than Morgan on his back.

"Fancy a night ride, Ava?"

"Absolutely!" she replied, climbing out the window and up Samphire's giant wing to sit behind Morgan.
"Where to?"
Ava whispered in his ear.
"Take me to my mother."

*Ava will return in **Time and Tide***

Appendix

The Thirteen

Timeline of Fae Ages

There are many who believe our human world is older than first thought. However, for the Fae this has always been the case. They have always believed that human historians got things wrong but then again, the Fae have always thought humans get everything wrong!

The world, our earth, is said to be 4.5 billion years old, so it has been here quite a while. Further, our human ancestors have been here for about six million years. Although modern humans evolved about 200,000 years ago, what about fairies?

This amazing world we live in keeps evolving and so do we, though changes take thousands of years. Fairies have evolved alongside humans, though in some form magic has been with the earth since its inception. Fairies too have been here for roughly 250,000 years, possibly longer as we have very little to go on. Remember, the first Writstars were not commissioned until the Age of Unicorn.

The very first Age, **the Age of Avalonia** is just a mystery to us as it is to our fellow friends, the Fae. However, what we do know is that most of the ancient spells and rituals stem from the Age of Avalonia as fairy priest and priestesses used to pass everything orally.

Though in fairy language orally meant 'wingly'. As the first fairies spoke only with their wings.

The Age of Avalonia truly was the beginning. The mythical King Thornang and Queen Bethning created a dynasty of peace and wonder.

We say mythical as the King performed such great feats of magic and wonder that no fairy could have been that powerful, but maybe he was? He was said to have commanded the stars of the heavens to show themselves and to speak so loud, the night sky would tinkle with the sound of twinkling stars.

It was said that fairies would dance all night to the sounds of heaven. He also told the moon to come down and bathe herself in the sea, as she was dirty from all the dust in space. As the moon shook herself dry and all the drops of water mingled with moon magic, and as they fell back into the water, the Mer people were created.

The Age of Avalonia is looked upon as a beautiful age full of wonderment, peace, and joy. Some young fairies of today look back at that age and try to recreate the carefree and happier existence of Avalonians. However, as fairies, they do dream and think of many strange things

The Age of Avalonia was a time before time. The Aborigine people of Australia described it best when they called it The Dreaming. A time of such magic and mystery that anything was possible. So much so that no element governed this Age.

In Fae time, as beings of nature, each Age is governed by an element which pre-determines the kind of fairies being born to that Age.

The five elements for humans are earth, air, fire, water, and Spirit or divinity. The five elements for fairies are earth, air, fire, water and the Universal Matrix.

However, in this Age, the Age of Avalonia, the

Universal Matrix was simply The Beginning. The beginning of all magical life as we know it. A time when pixies, Elves and the Mer people came into being. The race that crowned this time was the Fae.

After about 50,000 years the next Age that came into being was **the Age of Unicorn** which was governed by the element of earth.

It was said that the Age of Unicorn was truly magical, as this was the Age of the golden bluebell. These exquisite flowers are no longer to be found in the wild or anywhere as they are now quite extinct. Though perhaps this has something to do with how magical their properties were, and both Royalty and witches alike picked and used these plants until they were no more.

It was due to this extinction that a decree was made by the then ruling monarch that all plants and flowers be given special protection, and so wood nymphs became the guardians of nature. The decree also made sure that both witches and Monarchs have a special licence to use the powerful properties of plants.

The Age of Unicorn saw the rise of Leprechauns, Gnomes, Elves of the woods and forests, not to mention the nymphs and the Green Man. Further, the Age of Unicorn saw the birth of giants, trolls and ogres.

The Fae that were born at this time had green wings. These Fae were very practical and down to earth, that is probably why we find writing being developed in this Age. The Fae of this Age were rather disciplined for fairies, and everything was extremely methodical. We can still glimpse their magnificent monuments across the land with the white horses of the South Downs.

The Age of Unicorn also saw the alliance between the natural world and the magical one. Animals and insects worked alongside to bring about harmony, almost a symphony of sounds that drew upon the interconnectedness of all.

However, this synergy of togetherness was almost destroyed with the arrival of the next two ages.

The Age that followed the Unicorn was the **Age of Griffin.** This Age was governed by Air, so the elementals of Air took precedence over everything. Air is something that we do not see but need to survive just like magic itself. Air is invisible and this gave rise to the magical world becoming invisible.

Fae, Elves, Pixies, Mer people, Nymphs, Giants, Trolls and Ogres all could manifest the magic of the Age and its element, and therefore become invisible, and a great many did. As it is at this time also, we see the involvement of the human world which encroached into the magical kingdom.

It was deemed safer to be invisible to human eyes, by the ruling Monarchs, as so many Fae and other elementals had been captured by humans and used in spells and fairy tales.

It is worth a note here also concerning the Ages, for not only was each governed by an element but they were also overseen by the deities of that element. Therefore, in the Age of Griffin, for example the element of Air is governed by Hermes who had wings on his sandals, so he was able to fly here and there, causing mayhem and mischief. However, more shall be said on deities in the next chapter.

In this Age, Queen Leanna ruled in the first dynasty and hers was a great moment in Fae history as she brought with her creative inspiration.

Queen Leanna was known as Leanan Sidhe, pronounced Lanawn Shee, and was a native Irish air sprite. She was highly regarded in artistic circles, especially in the musical world.

The Age of Griffin saw not only the rise of musical and creative accomplishments but also the rise of Griffins, Air Sprites, the Sphinx and the Will o' the Wisp.

However, the Will o' the Wisp is often mistaken to be of the element of fire but he truly is one of the air elementals as he appears as a wispy, floating orb of white gas, giving an almost smoky illusion about him.

It was at this time, in the Age of Griffin, that a great many pieces of treasure were buried by Will o' the Wisp. However, it is said that not all the treasure was found and that is why to this day, Humans are still finding buried treasure in their gardens and land. This is because Will o' the Wisps buried everything they could find from gold to pottery, to jewels and crowns!

The Fae born in the Age of Griffin has yellow wings which represented the air. Whilst Royalty of this Age always had silver wings.

In the Age of Griffin, there was also a rise in the fairies of the air, in particular, the mist Fae, Tiddy Mun, but we shall visit his story further in the chapter on famous fairies.

The next Age to form on this timeline was **the Age of Dragon**. In the Age of Dragon, we see a rise in some of the most frightening beings of the enchanted realm.

The Age of Dragon, brought about of course, not only a rise in dragons and salamanders, but also the Banshee, an Irish death Spirit who is heard to wail with screams when a true Irish person is about to die. She is said to have fiery red eyes from her weeping but in truth no-one who has seen her has lived to tell the tale.

It is worth noting further that the Age of Dragon also saw the rise of the Djinn or Genie in our world. Though predominately in the Middle East, they found their way to us via humans who travelled on the ancient trade routes. The Djinn could manifest any wishes a mortal could desire but always at a cost. Genies are first and foremost tricksters, thus the need to keep these mischievous elementals at a distance is a must.

The Fae that were born in this Age had red coloured wings whilst Royalty had gold.

The Age we are in now is the **Age of the Selkie** as the water element prevails, that is why the human world in this Age is also affected. We either have too little water or too much. We know sea levels are rising and there are many storms which bring flooding. In this Age, we have also seen the rise of tsunamis and these are reminders that we need to live and work in harmony with the natural world.

The Age of Selkie has seen the rise of not only Selkies of course, but also the Undine, the Mer Folk and the Gwargedd Annwn, pronounced 'grageth anoon'. She is a

Welsh water sprite and is described as blonde and slender. We know her by another name and that is The Lady of the Lake. This wonderful being is gentle and wishes humans many blessings.

The Naiad and Nereid also prevail in the Age of Selkie. This is a very turbulent time we are living in, given the nature of the element that rules it.

Time and Seasons

In the world of Fae, time is eternal and cyclical. When a being lives for almost 10,000 years, time itself can stand still, and this is just one of the many secrets of the Fae.

In regards to this, Fae obviously have no need for watches or clocks as humans would understand. Instead there is a giant clock in the great hall at the heart of Avalonia. The clock, which is decorated so exquisitely, tells the Ages and includes the Royal Dynasties attached to them. It truly is a remarkable piece of engineering, and one in which not many humans have seen.

Yet this division between humans and Fae is blurred when it comes to the seasons, as both human and Fae alike are all affected by the natural world and its seasons.

The seasons for the Fae are marked, in particular, by the Festivals. For example, in the month that humans call June, the Fae call it Litha, after the festival which is of course, Midsummer.

Here is a list of the Fae months and the corresponding seasons and festivals.

Samhain (October-December)
Samhain is the beginning of a new year, although this occurs in the months October/November for humans, this is the most magical time of the year for Fae.

The actual festival or New Years' Day is Samhain and humans view this as Halloween, a mixture of scary and silly. It is silly but many Fae love it as it is a time to dress up and attend one of the many Samhain Masquerade Balls which are held at this time of year. Great feasting, fun and frivolity of all kinds are experienced. With the main colours being orange and black, many Fae turn up with tiger masks.

Samhain also sees Will O' Wisps' look for treasure. The Tiddy Mun also make an appearance. The Fog Fae are out in their droves across the Moors and Wolds of Lincolnshire and Yorkshire with many a naïve wanderer being in lost in their mysterious charms.

Yule (December – January)
This is another wonderful time of the Fae year for merry making and having fun. In fact, the Fae's year is full of opportunities to have parties which include lots of singing and dancing. One might say that is all a Fae year consists of, one giant party. Though it is true that Fae are very sociable beings and love meeting friends, playing dress up, having a Ball or several, they can be serious too, although not that often. When a fairy does become serious, their wings tend to fade.

Nevertheless, returning to Yule, this is a charming part of the year with winter well and truly under way. The large red berries on holly and hawthorn give way to the evergreens and ivy that grows in abundance.

There are many winter Balls with sumptuous meals, stout hearty broths and flowing acorn cups full of brandy wine and heather beer.

The festival they celebrate is Yule and similar to the human variety of Yule they celebrate the return of the King.

Traditionally the Fae King, from the new year till now, has been travelling the enchanted realm attending meetings and negotiating trade for the forthcoming year.

Also, in the time of Yule, many baby dragons are born. Some believe this is due to all the roaring fires that abound. Further, the Fae are particularly fond of the poem 'Twas the Night Before Yule' and often recite it the night before the actual festivities begin.

Imbolc (February - Beginning of March)
This is one of the most charming times of the year, one which the Fae absolutely adore. Imbolc is the season which brings the first signs of spring. In human terms, it is the months of February and March.

The Fae are eager for this time of year as clothes are changed from winter to spring colours, and all Fae love green. The green that appears is never seen again throughout the rest of the year. It is the fresh, young, spring green which is a light, lime, refreshing colour. The fairies love nothing more than flying past a spring hedgerow gathering all the different greens available.

This season brings the Fae fashion designers out and many new clothes of future seasons are exhibited. In fact, this time of year is the fashion extravaganza of the Fae world. Royalty and Fae from all corners of the globe descend on Avalonia, with many cultures and races enjoying the season with harmony and love.

The fashion parties are filled with beautiful foods of delicate spring flowers; crocus drops, snowdrop cake and hyacinth wine, not to mention the delicious Cawl and Bara Brith or speckled bread.

The first races are held, amongst them the Catkins Derby. All Fae are out in force for this day, wearing their finest spring attire. It is a sight to behold.

Ostara (End of March- Beginning of April)
The Fae often refer to this as the yellow month due to the daffodils, jonquils and yellow aconites that are out. The Fey towns and cities are awash with the colours of green, white and yellow with this festival.

Many Fae are wearing their spring greens whilst rebellious young ones are wearing daffodil yellows and the young Writstars, those who are new to their profession, wear white. As Writstars, every respect is given to them as they go about their daily chores. They are served first in shops and Fae Food Spas. The Fae do not have restaurants in the human sense of the term, instead they have a food spa.

The idea of somewhere to eat and then leave within a couple of hours is completely unknown in Fey. The process of eating is a special, social and joyous thing, therefore a food spa is where Fey go to spend all day eating, drinking and being indulged.

Ostara is also the traditional time of the year when Leprechauns, Brownies and hobgoblins are born.

Beltane (End of April – May)
This is a marvellous season and with it comes so much

colour. The rainbow Fae are out in force from the April showers, and the May flowers are brought forth, giving an abundance of colour explosions within the natural world. The Fae literally paint the whole world with colour at this time - red, yellows, blues, greens, purples, oranges, every colour imaginable can be in the May garden.

The festival itself is Beltane and is regarded as the fire festival of spring. Many salamanders are born at this time, along with a number of pixies, and of course flower fairies and their counterpart fire fairies, which are not often spoken of.

There are also magnificent spring Balls for this season and its glorious flowers. The Balls of this season are the magnificent masquerade Ball of the King and Queen who dress with all the finery that the season brings. Fantastic foods, glistening with May dew, give a diamond shine to everything. If ever there was a feast that looked truly magical then the spread for the Beltane Masquerade Ball held at the Palace of Dreams is the one. It is said that no human has ever witnessed one; it is only recorded by the Writstars on court documents that humans come to understand and know of it.

At the Ball, there is also a Maypole which young Fae use to fly round, looping the ribbons with time and space.

Litha (June-July)
The wonderful season of Litha or Midsummer, as humans call it, is the pinnacle of the year. There is so much to see, do, eat, drink and generally have as much fairy fun as

possible.

There are wonderful Midsummer Balls all over the kingdom and Fae and troll alike all partake in Midsummer Punch. This is a special beverage made with the flowers and nectar of the peach blossoms of the previous months. It is potent and even the smallest amount can send an average ogre into a deep sleep. So, it is recommended that only one small acorn cup can be used by the average fairy for this intoxicating drink.

Many games, races and fashion shows happen during this season, along with Fae marriages. Indeed, the present King and Queen celebrated their four thousandth wedding anniversary on a Midsummer in the human year of 1724.

Litha is a season to enjoy life, friends, family and food, and usually altogether.

This is also a season when the most baby Fae are born, though in the Age of Selkie many Mer Folk have also been born. The baby Fae of this Age are quite extraordinary looking, they are even more beautiful than the average fairy. They have big, blue eyes and exquisite blue wings that make a 'shooing' sound like the sea.

Lammas (August)
This is a rather melancholy season for the Fae. Even though it is in the height of the summer for humans, there is a change in the air. The highly sensitive Fae can sense this, and this season is the only time when a fairy can get sick. So, fairy doctors are usually very busy at this time of year, making sure all their patients are healthy and happy and

enjoying all the good things the world can give.

At this season, lots of bread and in particular Bara Brith is made, and in typical Fae fashion this time of year, a special type of Bara Brith is made - a sugar coated one. All this lovely fresh bread is washed down with plenty of honey wine which is often mistaken for mead but the two are completely different, just ask any weary traveller from the human world who is foolish enough to drink any or eat any of the speckled bread.

There are many parties of course and many pixies at this time of year celebrate Lammas by making their own form of Bara Brith, which is called Lammas bread. Many pixie households have their own traditional recipe for Lammas bread, but all include honey and sunflowers in some quantity.

Mabon (September)
Mabon is a beautiful season and is the second harvest festival of the year with Lammas being the first, hence the bread making.

Mabon is a sumptuous festival of the orchard harvest with apples, pears, plums and peaches all in abundance.

The harvest festivals and parties of the Fae go on for basically the entire month of September. Many games, sports, racing and fashion parades take place in the cities across the enchanted realm as the fruits of the earth are shown off and welcomed.

It is also a time when the first mushrooms make an appearance in the woods and forests, much to the fairies' delight. Many a good mushroom has found its way into a fairy's house to be used as new furniture for the coming winter. That is generally what fairies do, they never redecorate their houses, they just have new furniture, which is usually made from nature in some way, so in fairness it will need changing from year to year.

The festival of Mabon coincides with the Autumnal Equinox when each day is equal to night and is a very auspicious and magical time. There is a prophecy that a twice blessed child will make their appearance on this day and they will bring about a new dawn of awareness between the Fae and humans. No-one really knows for sure when this babe will be born which is usually the case with prophecy.

These seasons and festivals we have looked at are a remarkable window into the world of the Fae. Yet, there is a wonderful coincidence about them, as many humans are now beginning to follow these very same festivals. The witches have always followed them but many other traditions embraced these times of the year. Ostara, for example, which falls around the time of the Vernal equinox or spring equinox, found its way and crossed over into Christianity to become Eostre or Easter. A time of renewal and rebirth and resurrection.

Lammas has also been embraced as a harvest festival with bread being a part of the Christian service, giving thanks to nature. The Fae were pleased when they found out that, as they always thought humans did not care about nature and the environment, but in some small corners of the world there are pockets of change. It is these small, wonderful pockets of change that need to be nurtured and perhaps they will begin to pollinate other parts of the world with positive change for all who live within this earth. This is how the Fae think - that good thoughts and deeds are like seeds of a flower which need to be nurtured and then when the time is right the seeds fly off to seek other places to grow.

It is worth remembering that another name for fairies is The People of Peace.

Illustrations

The following illustrations are by the author, Flora-Beth Edwards. They show each member of The Thirteen and their lineage – that is, their family history, also known as their family tree. As an exercise, you might like to draw up your own family tree, see who are the heroes and the villains.

Aunt April Brevi
welsh
Mother of Wolf

Family Tree

April Morganna Breuil
B. 1932
Blackwood Wales

Isabella Dixon — M — George Syddle Breuil

Jerrard Dixon m Margaret Elbrighan

John Syddle Breuil m Mable Moffitt

Edward Dixon m Catherine Boutloel

Caleb Breuil m Mary Syddle

James Dixon m Morganna Gathrice

Robert Breuil m Ann Edwards

Peter Dixon m Angharad Jones

Sir William Breuil m Arwen Hughes

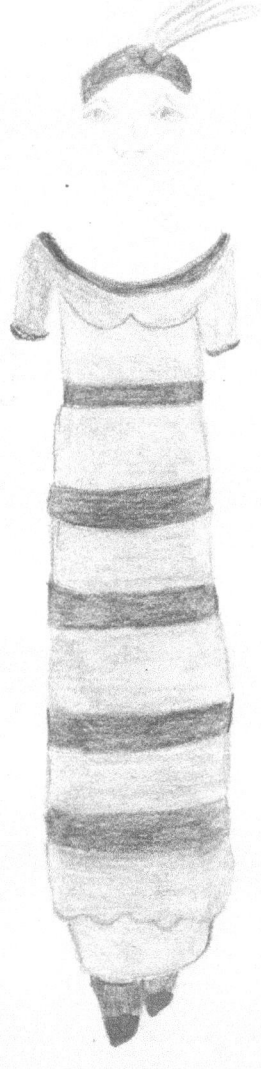

Aunt Brenna Monroe Killarney married to Aunt Fawn Grimstone

- Patrick Monroe M Sarah Foster
- Robert Finn M Catherine Parry
- Sean Monroe M Elizabeth Guthrie
- Billy Finn M Jane Foster
- John Monroe M Mary Atkinson
- Jacob Finn M Eleanor Curry
- Jack Monroe
- Bridie Finn
- Brenna Monroe, Killarney, Born: 1928 M Fawn Grimstone, Londonderry, Born: 1935

Aunt Briar Moffat

Single
Welsh
Artist

Briar Moffat
1932

Morgan

John Moffat (M) — **Elizabeth Morley**

Godfrey Moffat m Lydia Beeth	Thomas Morley m Constante Starr
William Moffat m Martha Rawson	Chrystopher Morley m Katherie de Moreby
George Moffat m Alexis Mussell	Richard Morley m Grace Neville
James Moffat m Frances Fanny Spedding III	Charles Morley m Ann West

Aunt Ellie Windrush
mother of Morgan
The Faery Codex
widow of Lord Seton

Elizabeth Windrush
Africa | Born: 1898

Mesi Abara   M   Kanye Windrush-
(water   Harrison
woman)   (Freedom)
| |

Lesedi Abara   Nikiruka M William
(woman of light)   (The greatest) Harrison
M   (will come)
Imamu Abara |
(Spiritual Leader)
| Thomas Harrison
Chike Abara   M
(Power of God)   Mary Partridge
M |
Delu Plautis
(The only daughter)   Joseph Harrison
| M
Beachy Head Woman   Bridget Ellen
Amara Grace
M
Cassius Aquillas Plautis
(Roman Centurion)

Rt. Hon. Lady Eowyn Labyrinth
1902
Penrith

Lewis Labyrinth — Lady Aeres Carter
m
Countess of Andrews

Osion Labyrinth
m
Pallaelia Atwood

Charles Carter
m
Beca Towne

Dylan, Lord of Penrith
m
Lady Alice Hankey

Edward Carter
m
Countess Blodwen of Trelawney

Baron Gruffydd
m
Josephine Montgomery

Sir Walter Carter
m
Lady Donna Fowell.

Aunt Fawn Grimsbone Londonderry Married to Aunt Brenna Monroe.

Fawn Grimsbane m Brenna Monroe
Londonderry   Killarney
Born: 1935   Born: 1928

Sean Grimsbane   Barbara King

Patrick
Kennedy-Grimsbane
m
Mary Burke

                                  Manus King
                                  m
                                  Bridget Lyndon

John Grimsbane
m
Katharine Kennedy

                                  Sir David King
                                  m
                                  Lady Marie of Lancashire
                                  Warrington
                                  Coates

Michael Grimsbane
m
Bridget Coyne

                                  Sir James
                                  Richardson
                                  m
                                  Lady Margaret
                                  Day

Family Tree

Guinevere Shadow
B: 1901
Caernarvon Valley

Afon Shadow m **Mary Sewell**

Aeron Shadow m Anouk Jones	Tobias Sewell m Anna Tubb
Cadfael Shadow m Donna Michaels	John Sewell m Eliza Renhdol
Deryn Shadow m Bladwyn Rose	David Sewell m Penny Edwards
Lord Edwyn Shadow m Lady Arwen Thomas	Issac Sewell m Lady Mary Moulson

Aunt Holly
Hart
Wiltshire
Single
loved a
Soldier —
missing in
Action

Holly Hart
Wiltshire, Born: 1945

James Hart	Ann Liddle
|	|
Robert Hart	Chrystopher Liddle
m	m
Agnes Wilson	Ann Bainbridge
|	|
William Hart	John Liddle
m	m
Hannah Whitehead	Frances Barton
|	|
Sir Ralph Hart	Timothy Liddle
m	m
Lady Catherine Hedworth	Elizabeth Smith

Aunt Ini Straleen
Welsh
Single
School Teacher

Ini Straleen 1922 Llyn Eiddwen

Lewis Straleen — M — Carys Thomas

- Eifion Straleen m Mary Flatters
- Huw Thomas m Alaw Williams
- Gawain Straleen m Meinir Lea
- Ifan Thomas m Donna Jacobs
- Glanmor Straleen m Nia Peterson
- Mabon Thomas m Iona Barnes
- Hedd Straleen m Angharad Davies
- Ninian Thomas m Eleri Edwards

Aunt Jissika Ataksak Mother of Chay

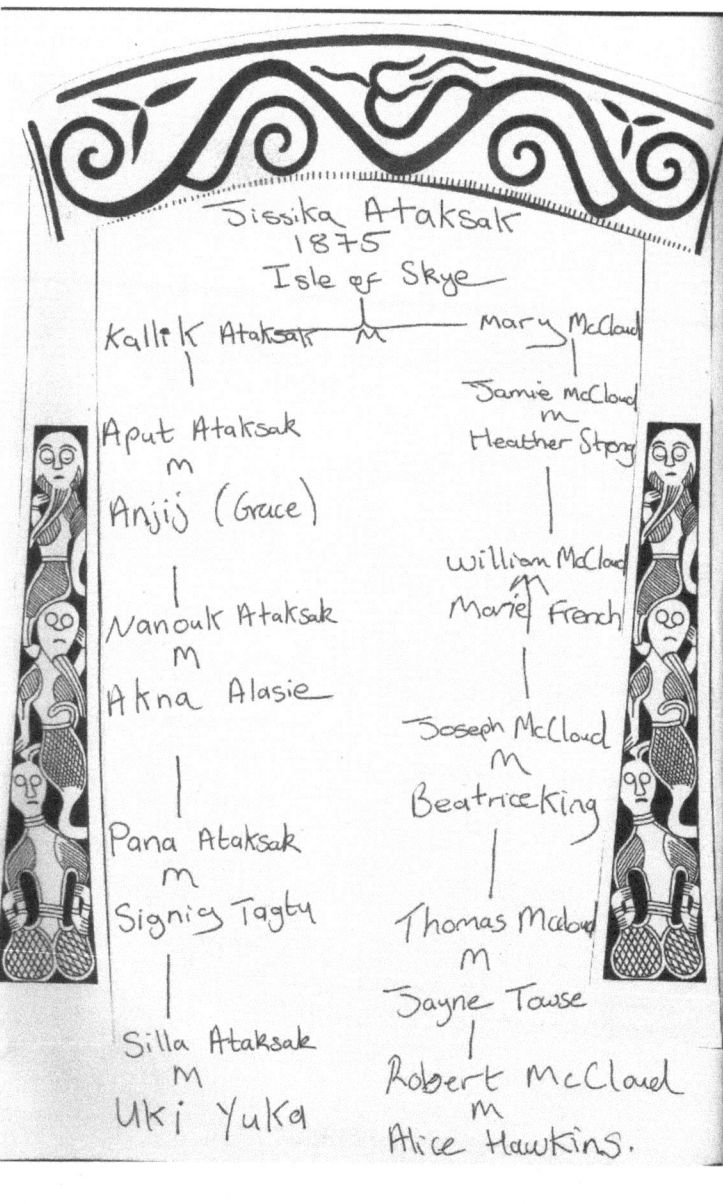

Aunt Lexi

The Faery Codex

Widow - Married a Sailor
missing in Bermuda Triangle

Alexia Thornton
Lincoln B: 1922

Aata Heketoro (Bear) **M** **Milicent Thornton**
(Fairy Spirit)
New Zealand

Aata Heketoro (Bear) (Fairy Spirit) New Zealand	Milicent Thornton
Akahata Heketoro (Supreme) M Anahera (majestic Angel)	Thomas Thornton M Susanna Wade
Kauri (The Great Tree) m Kaia (The Sea)	Wheatley Thornton M Ann Spibie
Ari (The Lion of God) m Maia (mother)	John Thornton M Sarah Lea Thompson
	Richard Thornton M Lady Isabella Browell

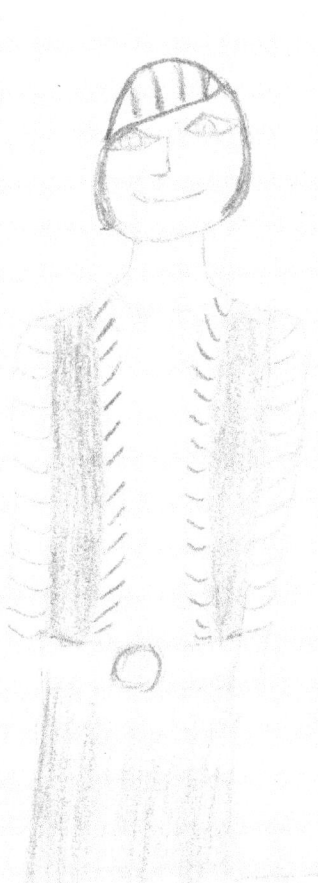

Aunt Meadow Pickering
Mother of Tarran English

Lady Meadow Pickering
1854
Salisbury

Lord Charles Pickering	Lady Ursula Waller

Peter George Pickering
m
Princess Joan Amados
|
Sir Grant Jacob-Pickering
m
Katherine Burnell
|
David Andrew Picking
m
Agnes Annesson
|
Lord Randolf Pickery
m
Lady Sophie
of
Penzance

Thomas Waller
m
Sarah Bacon
|
Lord Robert Waller
m
Elizabeth Tye
|
Sir Hugh Waller
m
Robina Goy
|
Sir Kenneth Waller
m
Lady Sarah Edwards

Aunt Winifred Wolfmoon Fellow

High Priestess and

Sister of Ava's Father

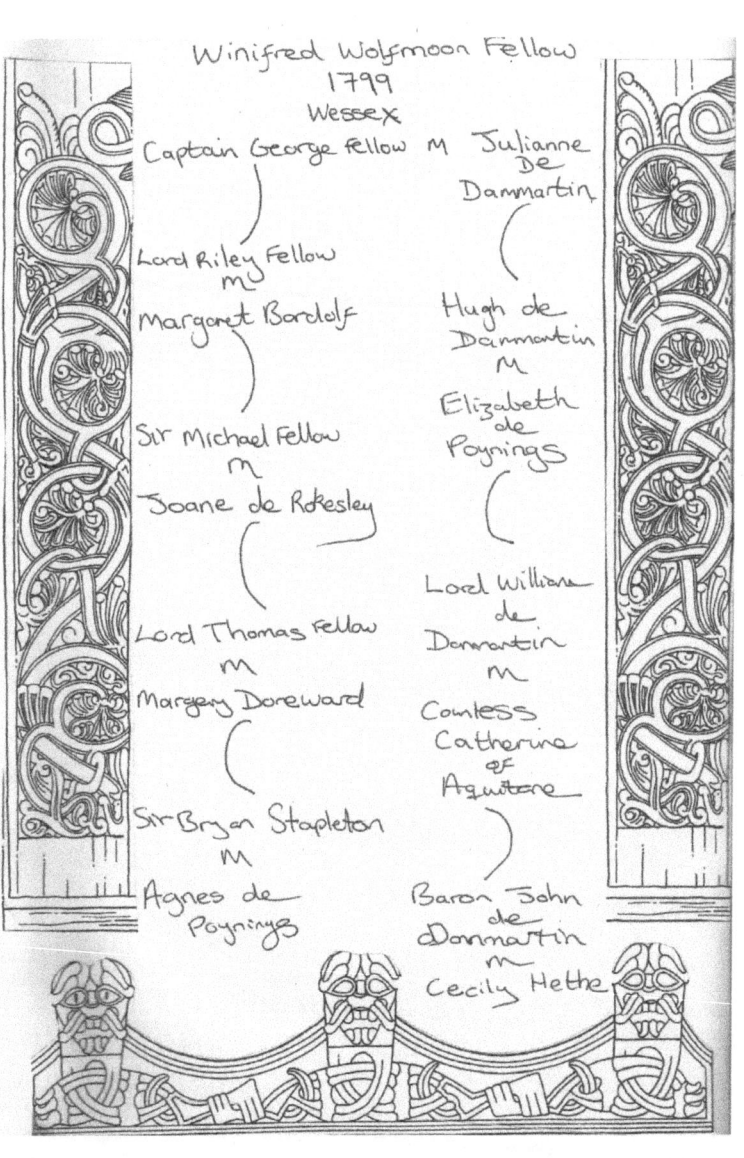

Winifred Wolfmoon Fellow
1799
Wessex

Captain George Fellow M Julianne De Dammartin

Lord Riley Fellow
m
Margaret Bardolf

Hugh de Dammartin
M
Elizabeth de Poynings

Sir Michael Fellow
m
Joane de Rokesley

Lord William de Dammartin
m
Countess Catherine of Aquitane

Lord Thomas Fellow
m
Margery Doreward

Sir Bryan Stapleton
M
Agnes de Poynings

Baron John de Dammartin
m
Cecily Hethe